T0354771

BEST FOOT

FOOT

FORWARD

BEST
FOOT
FORWARD

SCOTT LUDWIG

BEST FOOT FORWARD

iUniverse books may be ordered through booksellers or by contacting:

iUniverse
1663 Liberty Drive
Bloomington, IN 47403
www.iuniverse.com
1-800-Authors (1-800-288-4677)

ISBN: 978-1-5320-0720-0 (sc)
ISBN: 978-1-5320-0721-7 (e)

Print information available on the last page.

iUniverse rev. date: 09/16/2016

FOREWORD

There are two things you need to know about this book. First, it is the first book I've ever written specifically for a younger audience. Second, this is my first attempt at writing fiction. Believe me when I say that writing fiction is much more difficult than writing nonfiction. Why? We've all heard that if you tell lies it's really hard to keep them all straight. Well, writing fiction is like telling a whole bunch of lies and keeping all of *them* straight.

All of the characters, places and incidents have special meaning to me because they're based on my own personal experiences. For instance the main character, Jake Kerslake shares many of the qualities and characteristics of my long-time friend and running partner Al Barker. The name 'Jake' is the name my father called me his entire life and 'Kerslake' is the last name of the original drummer for Uriah Heep, one of my favorite bands when I was in high school. Jake's friend Jefferson Douglas is named for my two graduate school professors who introduced me to the sport of running, Thomas Jefferson Saine III and Douglas G. Bock. Blue Harbor Junior High's school colors are orange and blue, a tribute to my alma mater, the University of Florida. You may have noticed the shoes hanging on the bench on the front cover sport those two colors. This 'coincidence' is because the woman who designed the cover just so happens to be a member of the Auburn University family, whose colors are *also* orange and blue.

There are many more I could tell you about, but I'll just finish this up by reprinting two stories originally published in a couple of my earlier books. They will set the tone for the journey ahead.

KNOWING WHEN TO SAY YES

(Originally published in *Distance Memories: Reflections of a Life on the Run*)

'**N**o' will always be the safest answer. It's the easy way out. You're not committing to anything...or anyone. There's nothing for you to do, so you don't have to lift a finger. Follow up? None required.

But sometimes 'no' isn't the *right* answer. Many discover this to be true early in life; others later in life. I'm embarrassed to admit—I fall into the latter. It took less than a minute for me to realize it, although up until that moment I had been on this planet for over 53 years. Sixty seconds that had perhaps the most profound impact on my life was brought about by overhearing a conversation between strangers in the spring of 2008. I'll get to that story as soon as I provide a little background.

I've been a supporter of the March of Dimes since my first exposure to the organization during my junior year in high school. My friends and I decided to participate in the annual walk (at that time it was 20 miles) to raise money for this worthy charity. In all honesty the main reason we were doing it was to meet girls, the secondary reason being to listen to the various rock bands along the course. OK, we actually solicited for donations from some of our classmates and parents as well (after all that was the intent of the walk). We had a great time, heard some good music and raised a few dollars for a worthy cause (notice I didn't mention meeting any girls--that's because we didn't; we were much too shy in high school to talk to girls we didn't know).

When I began working for JC Penney Catalog in 1979, I noticed the company supported the March of Dimes and the United Way. I asked to organize a group of walkers for the 20-kilometer walk in the spring of 1980, and the event became an annual ritual for me and many of my fellow employees. I was the Chairman of our March of Dimes campaign for several years, and was proud to be in charge the year we set records with our fund-raising efforts. However, my rationale has changed since my junior year in high school; through working with the good people at the March of Dimes I have come to know and understand the challenges children with birth defects face each and every moment of their lives. To say they all are occupants of a very soft spot in my heart is an understatement.

It makes me sad to think about a newborn--who didn't ask to be brought into this world, as I used to tell my parents when I was upset with them--being burdened with a lifetime of physical, mental and/or emotional challenges before the moment they take their first breath on earth.

I have always been a supporter of the United Way as well, but I have to admit I'm pretty selective about which organizations I want my contributions to help. In 1992 JC Penney, Reebok and the United Way teamed up to support me in a 280 mile/six-day run across the state of Georgia (from Columbus to Savannah) as a fundraiser for the latter. Contributions were raised via a 'donation per dollar' campaign, and while I wasn't privy to the final tally for my efforts, I understand it was considered a success. I've always been proud of those six days of running--raising money for those that couldn't--along Highway 280 through the small rural towns of south Georgia.

Two really close friends of mine were blessed with a grandson, Jonathan. However, he was born facing the challenges of a life with spinal bifida. Jonathan was a fighter, and battling valiantly through a lifetime of hardships within the confines of a wheelchair, he was able to make it to his senior year in high school. However, he didn't live to see his graduation day. Jonathan would have graduated in May of 2008 from Liberty High School in Hinesville, Georgia. At the graduation ceremony, one of the speakers spoke about Jonathan--specifically, what a wonderful person he was--and presented Jonathan's parents with his diploma. My really close friends, Jonathan's grandparents were in the audience, and their tears of pride were soon followed by a spontaneous and unsolicited standing ovation from everyone else in the auditorium. I know my friends Sandra and Jack feel blessed to have had Jonathan in their lives.

One year after running in the Macon Labor Day Road Race I stopped in Griffin, Georgia at my favorite post-race fast food restaurant for lunch. As I was sitting at a table, I noticed a young lady with a noticeable limp----caused by one leg being considerably shorter than the other--sweeping the dining area and emptying the trash. She was undoubtedly one of the hardest-working people I've ever seen, and it was obvious she was taking a lot of pride in what she was doing. Several customers thanked her for taking the empty trays off their tables, and from the brief verbal exchanges I could tell the young lady had a noticeable stutter, which may have been the reason she appeared to be embarrassed by the nice comments spoken to her from strangers. I was so impressed by how hard she was working--and even *more* impressed by the gleam in her eyes as she surveyed the nice job she had done in the dining room, that I went out to my car to get the T-shirt I received for finishing the race and gave it to her, along with a $10 tip for demonstrating such a great work ethic and truly (I'm sincere when I say this) 'making my day.' She set her broom aside, gave me a hug and said 'thank you.' Those were the first two words I heard her speak without the slightest indication of a stutter.

One of the grocery stores in my neighborhood does a very noble thing. They make every effort to hire young adults with special challenges--most notably Down's syndrome--to specifically staff several areas of the store on Wednesdays. It's always a pleasure to pay for my groceries and see their smiling faces as I leave the store and hear them say 'have a nice day.' After that, I usually do. How could I *not?*

At the kickoff breakfast for a logistics convention in Chicago in May 2008, the keynote speaker was an executive from a major drug store chain who spoke of his pet project; a distribution warehouse in Anderson, South Carolina whose staff was partially comprised of physically, mentally and/or emotionally challenged individuals. Actually, 'partially' is an understatement, as 44% of the facility's work force was challenged in one way or another. The gentleman, Randy Lewis, explained he had an autistic son and that the dream of every parent with a handicapped child is to outlive their child by one day. His idea was to build a facility that embraced those facing the challenges of everyday life; to make them a vital and integral part of society; *to give them a chance.*

I was fascinated by his message, and listened intently to every word he said. I met Mr. Lewis afterward, and told him how impressed I was with him as a businessman and more importantly, as a human being. I asked if could arrange a tour of his Anderson facility several of my employees and I in the near future. He said it would be his honor for us to be his guests, and several weeks later I found myself and some of my staff getting the grand tour of his distribution center. I hadn't told my staff where we were going or why; only that this isolated warehouse in South Carolina was 'unique.' My employees instantly noticed the positive, constructive atmosphere. It would be much later before they realized that approximately half of the workforce was indeed 'unique,' and when they came across this discovery they were- -in a word--amazed. So was I. The pride and personal satisfaction on the face of every single employee of Randy Lewis' pet project... his vision...his dream was a breath of fresh air. He was a man who found it in his heart to take a stand, to say 'yes' to something when it would have been much easier to simply say 'no' rather than doing something about it.

Now, getting back to that conversation between strangers I mentioned earlier…

In the spring of 2008, our church undertook a project referred to as 'The Big Fix.' A single mother in the church and her two 20-something sons--all three mentally challenged--were facing eviction from their tiny two-bedroom home in Newnan, Georgia. My wife Cindy and I signed up to help in the project to essentially do a 'home makeover' so the family could continue to live in their modest abode.

Around noon, construction came to a halt so everyone could enjoy a lunch provided by several members of the church. Actually everyone living on the entire street enjoyed lunch, as the members literally went door-to-door offering meals as their way of saying thanks for letting us 'take over' the block, as our cars were literally lining both sides of the street. As Cindy and I were sitting on the curb, a woman of about 40 was pushing a stroller down the street and stopped to talk to two ladies sitting next to us. I recognized that the child--maybe a little over a year old--was facing the same challenges as my friends' grandson Jonathan. But there was something else about him I couldn't put my finger on.

The woman went on to tell the two ladies she was a foster mother for the boy until she found parents willing to adopt him. She explained the youngster was born with cerebral palsy, and that doctors had informed her they had recently discovered the child was also totally blind.

Before I knew it I was crying. Not sobbing, mind you, but openly and uncontrollably crying. I didn't know why.

Cindy put her arm around me and asked 'Do you want to take him home?'

My heart said yes. Oh, how my heart said yes. But I couldn't speak. All I could do was shake my head. Not up and down, but left to right. My heart said 'yes' but my mind said 'no.'

When Cindy asked me 'Do you want to take him home' a thousand different thoughts bounced around in my head. *How much care the child would need; how much I wanted to make a difference in his life; how little time I had for him with a full time job, two sons of my own, the task of settling up the estate and affairs of my parents who had passed away several months earlier; how much I know Cindy would be the perfect mother for him; could I possibly be a father to an infant when I was already 53 years old...and would either one of us even be able to toss a baseball around in the back yard in 10 years...*

But the only thing I had to show for it was a nod. A side-to-side nod indicating 'no.'

I was disappointed in myself. I had taken the easy way out. But yet I still couldn't understand what was making me cry.

I later read the autobiography of golfing great Ken Venturi. Once Mr. Venturi's golfing career was over he became one of the finest golf commentators in the history of television. His announcing partner for many years, Jim Nantz, wrote the Foreword for the book. Contained in the Foreword was the most beautiful, heart-wrenching and soul-awakening sentence I have ever read:

> *Tom Pernice Jr. won the 2001 International Golf Tournament at Castle Pines and Kenny broke down and cried when young Brooke Pernice, born with a disease that causes blindness, touched her daddy's face in search of his smile.*

It was the first time I ever cried reading a book, and I now understood what had made me cry one spring afternoon taking a lunch break on a curb in Newnan, Georgia.

It was because I didn't have the courage to say yes.

MELISSA: A STORY OF A CHAMPION

(Originally published in *Running through My Mind:
Confessions of an Every Day Runner*)

I went to Warm Springs one hot summer night in June of 2001 to run a race sponsored by the Roosevelt Warm Springs Institution for Rehabilitation. The Institution works with 5,000 people annually with various disabilities. The race was to raise money for the seated and mobility clinic; in other words, children and young adults confined to wheelchairs.

Prior to the 10K race, a shorter race of 2K was held for the youngsters who were clients of the clinic. I watched one little girl who couldn't have been more than 10 years old nor weigh more than sixty pounds push the tires on her wheelchair so hard that she almost won the female division of the race. She finished a close second to a young lady who was much older, bigger and stronger than she was. But I promise you she didn't go down without a fight, struggling so hard on that final uphill with everything she had in hopes of passing that one last competitor.

After all the wheelchair-bound children had completed their race, the 'able-bodied,' as the starter called them, competed in theirs. The field wasn't too deep, and I managed to win the Men's Masters (40 years and older) division.

At the awards ceremony, trophies were awarded to the winners of the wheelchair race first. 'Melissa,' as I discovered the tiny girl's name to be, was called to the stage. Melissa wheeled up the ramp to the stage to receive her second place trophy, six inches of metal and marble which made her break out in a big smile. I noticed her mother in the crowd with a smile even bigger than her daughter's.

Afterwards, awards were presented to the 'able-bodied,' and I was called to the stage to receive my trophy which was – and I am not exaggerating – three feet tall! It made me think about the effort I put out for *my* race, and then about the effort Melissa had put out for *hers*, and I realized who the TRUE champion was. I looked where Melissa and her mother had been in the audience but didn't see them. I went to some of the people in that vicinity and they told me Melissa and her mother had left. Fortunately they were able to point me in the direction they had headed.

I found them just as the mother had gotten Melissa seated in the back of their van, and noticed Melissa was still holding onto her trophy for dear life. I introduced myself and said I had won the Master's competition, and asked Melissa if she would do me the honor of accepting MY trophy, as HER effort that evening had been much greater than mine and that she was the *real* champion. Melissa broke into the biggest smile I have ever, and I do mean EVER seen and she immediately pried the engraved plate off of her trophy, did the same to mine, and placed HER plate on her *new* trophy! I felt honored that Melissa accepted, and I knew by the tears running down her mother's face that she was OK with it as well.

I asked Melissa if I would see her at the race next year, and she told me she would be and that *she* was going to win a trophy for *me*!

And do you know what? I've already selected a spot on the mantel for it.

DEDICATION

For Jonathan, Melissa
and one special little boy whose name I never knew

…and for Allison.

CONTENTS

ONE – THE PITTS

....

Sooner or later it was bound to happen.

But what else would Jake Kerslake--whose notoriety around Blue Harbor Junior High was divided between his tendency to stammer over words beginning with the sound of a hard 'K' and his thin legs more appropriate for a praying mantis than a fourteen-year old boy—expect? After all, when you're only five-foot-two and 94 pounds in ninth grade, you're not simply another student. You're much more than that. You're a target.

Jake was running as fast as he could with a 12-pound backpack slung across his shoulder to avoid what had become a daily ritual after the final bell at 3:30. For most of the students it signaled the end of another school day. For kids like Jake it signaled the beginning of the daily edition of 'The Pitts,' featuring the designated target of the day. The rumor around school had been that today was going to be Jake's day, and he wanted no part of it.

Here's how 'The Pitts' worked. The Blue Harbor 'Brat Pack,' comprised mostly of the muscular behemoths who were too uncoordinated to make the JV football team would wait in the school parking lot at the end of the day for their target--in this case Jake—to make an appearance. The Brat Pack, with 200-pound, 16-year old Tim Pittsinger (his advanced age due to having repeated both the third and fourth grades) calling the shots, would encircle their prey and take turns shoving him from one Brat Packer to another, sometimes for as long as 15 minutes. Several weeks earlier the target was tiny Kenny Dailey, who succumbed to the rigors of 'The Pitts' in a matter of only two or three minutes. Kenny took the easy way out; he fainted, allegedly due to dizziness but more likely due to the sheer fear of being pushed around like a rag doll by a half-dozen boys, all of them at least twice his size.

But today was going to be different because Jake had no intention of being the Brat Pack's 'monkey in the middle.' Jake decided that once the school bell sounded signaling the end of the day, he was going to run.

And run he did. Jake not only outran the entire Brat Pack but several members of Blue Harbor's cross-country team who were running on the sidewalk on the opposite side of the street as well. Jake was running so fast--his arms pumping furiously and his face turning a shade of red that was actually closer to burgundy--that he caught the attention of cross-country coach Bill Rose who was peddling furiously behind his team on his Pee Wee Herman bicycle; yes, the one the entire student body of Blue Harbor ridiculed him for riding but no one dared to say a word about.

However, Coach Rose was not the only one watching. Jefferson Douglas, or 'JD' as he was known when he was Jake's age many, many years ago was watching as well, his bloodshot eyes peering from beneath yesterday's newspaper from his spot on the park bench. JD caught a glimpse of the graceful yet efficient running motion of young Kerslake as he outran his pursuers as easily as a gazelle might outrun a Zamboni. JD knew he would bet his last dollar—if in fact he had a dollar in his pocket—that the Brat Pack would never outrun the boy with the legs of a praying mantis. Not today, not tomorrow, and in all likelihood not *ever*.

After all, if there's one thing other than which restaurant had the best food scraps at the end of the day that JD knew about, it was running.

And this boy Kerslake could *run*.

TWO — COACH ROSE

The suspense of being the focus of 'The Pitts' the next day was short lived because Jake would be somewhere else after school other than the parking lot. At 3:30 he was asked to stop by Coach Rose's office, an invitation every boy at Blue Harbor knew was one they weren't able to refuse. Rumor has it that many years ago one brave eighth grader skipped out on a 3:30 meeting with Coach Rose and was never seen nor heard from again. The fact that his father got a promotion at work and his entire family moved to San Diego had absolutely no bearing on what actually happened, because at Blue Harbor Junior High rumors had a life of their own. In other words Blue Harbor was just like any other school.

Jake didn't know what was behind the invitation. He wondered if word had gotten around about how he went out on a limb and told his small but close-knit group of friends Coach Rose's bicycle really *was* the one Pee Wee Herman used to ride. No, that couldn't possibly be the reason. If it were, Coach Rose would need a room larger than his closet-of-an-office to accommodate everyone in school guilty of the same offense. There was barely enough room to display the pair of county championship trophies his teams had won over his 36-year coaching career, let alone a couple hundred students who all referred to him as 'Pee Wee' behind his back.

Jake stood outside Coach Rose's office, his heart beating as fast as it had been about 24 hours earlier when he was outrunning the entire Brat Pack and half of the cross-country team. Coach motioned for him to enter and before Jake pulled the office door shut behind him he was hit with a barrage of questions.

'How long have you been running?'

'Do you have any idea how fast you are or how far you can run?'

'Have you ever thought about RUNNING FOR YOUR SCHOOL?'

Jake explained he'd been running as long as he could remember and that he had no idea how fast or how far he could run. But he did say he couldn't ever remember getting tired while running: That much he knew for a *fact*.

'I don't know how far or how fast I c-c-c-can run, but I know I c-c-c-can beat the school bus home most afternoons. Especially if I'm in a hurry to catch the C-c-c-creature Feature on Channel 6 at 4:00 p.m. when there's something special on. The original 'Godzilla,' for example. I leave school at 3:30 and run directly home; on a good day I c-c-c-can be on the c-c-c-couch in my living room in time to see the opening c-c-c-credits.'

Jake said he played lots of sports growing up, but there weren't any he was particularly good at. In fact there weren't any sports he could even live up to the modest billing of simply being 'adequate.'

He played Little League Baseball and had the speed on the base paths to stretch a line-drive single to the outfield into a standup double. The only problem was Jake was never able to hit the ball into the outfield. In fact Jake rarely made contact with a pitched ball and when he did the best he could do was dribble a feeble foul ball down the first base line.

Bantam football? Jake played wide receiver for the first couple of games because the coaching staff knew he could run like the wind. The only problem was Jake couldn't catch a football if it was hand-placed into his arms and coated with Super Glue.

In eighth grade Jake tried out for the school basketball team. There wasn't a player on the team who could keep up with Jake when someone passed him the ball on a fast break. The only problem was Jake couldn't make a shot even if the basket was as wide as the Mississippi River.

Three sports, three one-and-done's. He never gave sports like tennis and golf a chance: There was just too much hand/eye coordination required with little need for running, the only thing he was good at.

But no, Jake never thought about running for his school. There were just too many problems.

But Coach Rose had other ideas. He told Jake he could envision him wearing the uniform of the Blue Harbor Herons, with one mission and one mission only:

Cover the path in front of you to the best of your ability.

There would be no need for bats, balls and baskets; but rather a strong spirit, a healthy heart and all the desire and determination a fourteen-year old boy could muster. From what he had seen the previous afternoon, Jake appeared to have all the bases covered.

Jake left Coach Rose's office with two pairs of running shorts, two singlets and a warm-up suit in the orange and blue of the Blue Harbor Herons.

Not to mention a smile on his face as wide as the Mississippi River.

Jake would indeed be running for his school.

THREE – JEFFERSON DOUGLAS

Jake was carrying more than usual in his backpack with the addition of his new orange and blue running attire, but that didn't stop him from running home faster than the day before when he was being pursued by the Brat Pack. Jake wasn't accustomed to anyone complimenting him on his physical abilities. Being asked to be part of a team whose success is measured solely by the purest of physical efforts was all the motivation he needed to run home so fast that he knew he would have time to fix a peanut butter and jelly sandwich and a glass of ice cold milk before *Jurassic Park* filled the screen in his living room.

So fast, in fact Jake barely heard the words 'excuse me' in a voice he had never heard before as he was running along the sidewalk—'the path in front of him,' Coach Rose had called it--at a pace so fast he could hear the breeze as he ran. Maybe what Jake heard was just the wind playing tricks with his mind. Or perhaps it was Tim Pittsinger hiding in one of the bushes running parallel to the asphalt, hoping for the chance for a little 'one on one' with Jake. Either way, Jake stopped to ask the elderly gentleman he had noticed sitting on the park bench in front of Central Park for the past week or so if he had seen anyone.

The old man replied: *'You're the only person I've seen in several hours. Truth be known I barely saw you, you were moving so fast. You've got quite the gift there.'*

Jake explained he thought he had heard someone say 'excuse me.'

'Guilty as charged. The name is Jefferson Douglas, but my friends call me JD. I don't have many. Friends, that is. But the ones I have are very special to me. How about you calling me JD and I'll make you a promise: I'll call you

'friend' and do everything in my power to help make you the fastest runner you're capable of being. I can promise you that.'

Jake's eyes examined the elderly gentleman from head to toe. Jake wondered if an old man sitting on a park bench, with a newspaper in one hand wearing a shirt tattered with holes would still be considered a 'gentleman.' Jake also wondered what this tired old man could possibly know about running. Jake noticed the torn and faded orange T-shirt the man was wearing had 'BEST FOOT FORWARD' in bright blue lettering across the chest. Jake asked the significance of the three words.

'I used to run some myself, so I know a little bit about it. One thing I knew back when I was your age and I still remember to this day: Whether it's running or in life, you always have to put your best foot forward. I know it may not look like it to you, but I've lived by those words every single day of my life.'

Jake reached out to shake the hand of his new friend. Maybe it was a gut feeling, maybe it was the catchy three-word slogan or maybe it was just the pair of worn out running shoes tied together and hanging from the corner of the park bench that may or may not belong to the gentleman. Regardless of the reason why, Jake called the old man 'JD' for the first time.

And just like that Jake--JD's newest friend--had taken the first step towards becoming the fastest runner he was capable of being.

And unbeknownst to Jake, making what would become a lifelong friend.

Had Jake been paying attention he might have noticed the blue Chevy Impala passing by Central Park with Coach Rose behind the steering wheel. Coach had been impressed by the comment Jake made about 'being home by 4:00 p.m.' Knowing that Jake could make the run from school to his house in 30 minutes, he was curious to find out how far it was. So he made the drive from the front of the school to the Kerslake's house with a watchful eye on the car's odometer. It displayed 134,481.0 miles when he left school. As he passed by Jake's driveway he noted the new number on the odometer: 134,486.4. Amazing! Jake was capable of running 5.4 miles in less than 30 minutes! Not to mention while wearing a backpack.

'That boy was wrong about being able to run,' Coach thought to himself. *'That boy can FLY.'*

FOUR - JESSICA

Most people wouldn't be able to recognize Jake was running with more 'spring in his step' than usual.

But Jessica Martin wasn't 'most people.' Rather, she was literally the girl-next-door who had been secretly in love with Jake since the day he rescued her white kitten Maui when the two of them were in second grade. Maui had climbed to the top branch of the oak tree in the Martin's front yard before realizing he knew a lot more about climbing up than he did climbing down. Fortunately Jake Kerslake, savior of cats, was living right next-door and available to save the day. Today Maui is 10 pounds heavier than he was on that fateful day, but Jessica's secret crush on Jake remains as strong as ever.

Yes, Jessica could tell something was different in Jake so she made her way to the sidewalk to greet him and ask about his day.

Jake had no trouble telling his BFF ('best friend forever') about what had transpired.

'C-c-c-coach Rose asked ME to run on the c-c-c-cross-c-c-c-country team. He thinks I c-c-c-can be a really, really good runner. He believes in ME!'

Jake tore open his backpack to show Jessica the orange and blue uniform he would be wearing to represent his school. He had trouble containing his excitement; Jessica smiled on the inside as she remembered the first Christmas she shared with Jake and how excited he was opening up the package containing his very first Teenage Mutant Ninja Turtle figurine. In some strange way it gave today the feeling of Christmas, even though the actual holiday was still over ten months away.

Jake told her just about everything. After all, that's what BFF's do. Everything, that is except meeting his new friend JD.

It wouldn't be long, however before JD would be adding Jessica to his small yet intimate circle of friends.

FIVE — PARENTS

Now for the real test: What would Jake's parents think?

Former high school sweethearts, David and Alice Kerslake had both become prominent figures in the small city-by-the-sea of Blue Harbor. Although they were both graduates of the University of Florida, they quickly adapted to the ocean side lifestyle Blue Harbor had to offer. David was the founder and owner of Kerslake's Hardware, a position in the community he parlayed into a four-year term as Mayor of Blue Harbor right after Jake was born. Alice was the Vice Principal of Blue Harbor Elementary, foregoing the opportunity to take over as Principal when Old Man O'Reilly retired just about the same time she gave birth to her baby boy almost 14 years ago to the day. Alice never looked back on her decision; rather she enjoyed watching her son develop as a scholar as they co-existed in the same building during Jake's first six years in public education.

The Kerslake's had always been very protective of their only child. To say that Jake's three months of playing football was the toughest period of their lives would be an understatement. Every game, every practice, every snap of the ball they knew there was the distinct possibility their small-framed son had a legitimate chance of getting hurt—and hurt badly—playing a game involving intense physical contact with other boys twice his size. Jake's one season of both baseball and basketball was no picnic for them either.

But tonight their reaction would be honest, sincere and from the heart. They knew their son could run. They knew their son *loved* to run. Most of all they knew running didn't involve any physical contact against boys twice their son's limited stature. Jake's news of being asked to run on the cross-country team truly made them happy... because they could see it made *Jake* happy.

Judging from the smiles on their faces and the pride in their eyes, it was evident Jake had the full support of the two most important people in his life.

There was nothing left to do but lace up his shoes and run ... on whatever path was in front of him.

SIX — DAY ONE

I t was easy to spot the newest member of the Blue Harbor cross-country team.

Aside from the usual tell-tale signs—a smile on his face stretching from ear to ear and more spring in his step than a jackrabbit—there was the laser-like focus in his eyes as Jake listened to every word, observed every gesture and absorbed every emotion of Coach Bill Rose.

Just before he sent the team out for their afternoon workout he called Jake to his side for an announcement: *'Before we get out there I want to introduce Jake Kerslake. If I'm not mistaken Jake intends to introduce all of you to his backside once we start pounding the asphalt this afternoon.'* His comments excited the team, as evidenced by how many boys were trying to squeeze through the tiny four-foot wide doorframe at one time. They were all eager to get outside and run; the sooner the new kid could see that respect had to be *earned* to be called a true Blue Harbor Heron the better.

Jake took off running like the wild hyenas the students had seen chasing after their prey in an old black-and-white film in Mr. Muldrow's third period science class. Only in this case there was no prey; only the empty path in front of him. The rest of the team—maybe 20 boys in all—were spread out over half a mile less than 30 minutes into the run; the closest runner to Jake was at least a couple of football fields behind as he reached the bright orange plastic cone on the edge of the sidewalk indicating the turnaround point. Jake circled the cone and began retracing his steps back to the school gymnasium. A mere five miles into his very first run as a Heron, the memories of his prior athletic failures were fading from sight in the rear view mirror in his mind.

With little more than a mile remaining—and sporting a lead of at least a quarter of a mile over a relentless, never-say-die Eric Shay, Jake's confidence was at an all-time high. Jake thought for a brief moment of being the first one on the team back in the locker room when the strangest thing happened: He was losing control of his legs. He was still moving forward—still maintaining a rather fast pace—but he was no longer running in a straight line. It was as if both of his legs had minds of their own and weren't able to agree on which direction to go. It was only a matter of time before Eric Shay had Jake in *his* rear view mirror.

As the team slowly reassembled—one tired runner after another-- inside the cramped quarters of the Blue Harbor Junior High boy's locker room, a dejected Jake Kerslake grabbed his towel and headed to the shower room, only to be momentarily stopped by Coach Rose.

'Jake, I was proud of you today. You ran with your heart. Soon you'll be running with your head. Do you know what you did today? You started out with a bang and ended with a whimper. Tomorrow we're going to reverse that: You're going to start out with a whisper and finish with a scream. Go home and get some rest; it won't be long before the world meets Jake Kerslake the runner.'

Jake showered in silence as he tried to make sense of what had just happened. His legs had never failed him like that before. Then again he had never put them through a run like that before, either. As he toweled off he wondered to himself what Coach Rose meant when he said he would have him 'running with his head.'

'What's wrong with running with my heart?' Jake whispered to no one in particular.

SEVEN – THE FIRST WEEK

J ake couldn't understand it.

In his heart he believed he had the most speed and endurance of anyone on the team yet he had still not been the first one back in the locker room after an entire week of practice. Actually Jake *did* understand it; he just didn't want to recognize it.

Fortunately for Jake, JD was there to clear things up.

It was Friday evening and Jake, not the type of person to spend his free time in a movie theater or game arcade like most of the kids in ninth grade, was spending some time alone in Central Park thinking about his first five runs as a member of the Blue Harbor Herons. Specifically he was thinking about Coach Rose reminding him he had the physical attributes, the talent and the desire to be one of the finest runners the school had ever produced. *'But until you learn how to think like a runner, you'll never reach your full potential.'* Coach Rose's words stung as much floating around in his mind tonight as they did the first time he heard them.

Jake was in a fog as he paced the two-mile asphalt path around the perimeter of the park. The deep voice of Jefferson Douglas—as soft and velvety-smooth as the Barry White CD's his parents listened to—caught Jake completely by surprise.

'I've been watching you and your teammates run by here every day this week. Actually I've seen you two times each day; once coming and once going. Do you know what I've seen? A boy with all the talent in the world…and absolutely no idea of what to do with it. THAT'S what I've seen this week.'

While JD's voice caught Jake by surprise, his words had an even greater impact.

They stung. It was the same comment he had heard earlier from Coach Rose.

Jake immediately put himself on the defensive. *'I've led the team for at least eight of the 10 miles we ran on Monday and Wednesday. I ran my first six 800's faster than anyone else on Tuesday; so what if I pulled up the rear on the last two? On Thursday I had a great practice if you don't c-c-c-count the timed mile we ran at the very end. And today was just a c-c-c-casual five mile run to k-k-k-keep the juices flowing, according to C-c-c-coach Rose. There was no need to push it.'*

JD pounced on Jake's comments like a ravenous lion might pounce on a three-legged zebra.

'You don't want to play 'so what' with me, my friend. So what if you didn't finish first? So what if you pulled up the rear? So what if you discount the mile at the end? Do you see a common theme here? You're convincing yourself it's acceptable not to give your absolute best. All you're doing is lying to yourself. Don't you realize you're throwing away your talent? Don't you realize you're throwing away your GIFT?'

Jake had never thought of his ability to run as a gift. He knew he wouldn't be able to get that thought out of his head the entire weekend if he didn't do something about it.

'Can you be here in the morning, JD?' I want to sleep on what you said, and then tomorrow I want to pick your brain. How about it?'

'I'll be here. I have no place else to be.'

'Then it's a date. How does seven a.m. sound?' Jake couldn't wait.

'Make it six.' Neither could JD.

EIGHT - MELISSA

Jake woke up on Saturday morning well before the 5:15 a.m. alarm he had set the night before. Excited about the prospects of hearing earth-shattering and life-changing advice from the man who thought his running was—a *gift*—it never dawned on him how impressed his parents were that he had turned in for the night a couple of minutes after 9 p.m.

On a Friday night, no less.

Jake threw on an old warm-up suit and laced up his oldest pair of running shoes that were now used for nothing more than mowing the yard and washing the family cars. He thought the attire appropriate for spending the frosty morning sitting on a park bench and 'talking shop' with his newest fan.

'Don't get comfortable. We're going for a little walk.'

Jake was a little confused. He arrived in Central Park with a cup of coffee for JD in one hand and a cup of hot chocolate for himself in the other as he thought they would be sitting on the bench to talk about how talented Jake was and that he was the best thing in running since the invention of the waffle sole training shoe.

'Is that for me?' JD asked as he wrapped his hand around the cup of piping hot coffee. Jake noticed every finger in JD's hand were twisted and contorted, similar to one of the characters—*Igor, that was his name!*—from one of the Creature Features on Channel 6 he had seen the other day.

'That's a mighty fine cup of coffee. Let me guess; your mom's handiwork?'

'No, actually I woke up early and made it myself. Guess I did OK-K-K-K, huh?'

JD mumbled something unintelligible beneath his breath. Jake took it to mean 'yes.'

They walked for the better part of 20 minutes on the sidewalk into town side-by-side, step-for-step in total silence. If it weren't for the occasional 'sluuuurp' as they sipped from their plastic cups, the squirrels and chipmunks of Central Park wouldn't have even known they were there.

Suddenly JD stopped in front of the large plate glass window at the front of Happy Burger, one of the favorite after-school hangouts for the cool kids in town. JD carefully examined the trash receptacles lining the front of the store before tossing his empty cup into the one labeled 'Plastic.' Jake made a mental note of how much JD had to squint his eyes in order to find the correct receptacle. This in turn caused him to wonder why JD wouldn't simply ask him and save the obvious strain on his eyes.

It also made Jake wonder if the two of them would ever really become friends or if JD would be the confidant and mentor he was hoping for. *'Give it time,'* Jake mumbled beneath his breath.

Jake noticed JD's eyes were focused on a young girl with a broom in her hand and a washrag tucked into the waist of her Happy Burger blue pants. She couldn't have been more than 15. Jake noticed everything about her: Hair pulled back in a tight ponytail, a radiant smile accompanied by a gleam in her crystal blue eyes... and one shoe with a sole visibly larger than the other. Walking was obviously difficult for her as she moved with a noticeable limp from table to table.

JD looked over at Jake and asked him simply: *'What do you see?'*

Jake wasn't sure how to answer. He didn't want to point out her physical shortcoming; that would be rude. He didn't want to point out her pretty face; he didn't want JD to get the wrong impression. He didn't know *what* to say.

JD didn't give him long to answer. *'Let me tell you what I see, Jake. I've known her since she was six years old. Her name is Melissa. She was born with one leg four inches shorter than the other, so she's been dealing with that limp you see her entire life. She is a fighter. She doesn't have many friends in school—in fact I bet you don't even know she goes to your school, Jake—but she doesn't let that get her down. But besides being a fighter and a friend of mine, do you know what I like most about her?'*

Again, Jake didn't know what to say. He thought it best to let JD answer his own question.

'The young lady takes pride in what she does. You can see it in her face, in her eyes and in her smile as she goes from table to table doing the absolute

best job she is capable of doing, making sure each and every one of the tables is spotless so each and every customer will have the best dining experience possible. The pride she takes in her work…well, it makes me proud to call her my friend. Would you like to meet her?'

Jake lifted his chin from his chest, nodded slightly and followed JD as he opened the front door to Happy Burger and walked inside.

'Hi, JD! You're up early this fine Saturday morning! Can I get you your usual?'

Jake couldn't believe he had never heard Melissa's melodic voice in the halls of Blue Harbor Junior High before.

'This is my new friend Jake Kerslake. Jake, meet Melissa, one of my oldest friends.' Now JD was the one who was beaming with pride.

'Nice to meet you, Melissa.' Jake's voice was barely above a whisper.

'Jake Kerslake! My family lives on Oak Harbor Lane, the street right behind the one you live on. I see you running home from school all the time from my seat on the bus. It's so great to finally meet you!'

Jake had a hard time maintaining eye contact. His mind was deliberating on what he was feeling at that exact moment. This wasn't his first time in Happy Burger and he had *not once* thanked Melissa for making it a clean place to eat; in fact he had never even so much as said hello to her.

Suddenly it hit him like a ton of bricks.

He knew *exactly* how he felt and the feeling stayed with him once he got home and lasted throughout the night.

Ashamed.

NINE — HERO OF THE DAY

Sunday morning wasn't quite as welcoming as Saturday had been. Still licking his wounds from yesterday's long overdue and somewhat embarrassing introduction to Melissa, Jake couldn't figure out what to do. So he did what he normally did when he needed some time to sort things out.

He went for a run.

His normal running route took him on the sidewalk encircling Central Park, a moderate five-mile route that ordinarily took him a half hour or so to complete. When he was feeling particularly energetic and/or needed some time to be alone with his thoughts, he added a six-mile stretch through town that lengthened his route to 11 miles. Today was one of those days—he wanted some time alone—so he took the right turn onto Fletcher Street that took him right through the heart of Blue Harbor, the small town where everybody seems to know your name.

As Jake was running through town he wondered how he never came to know Melissa's name. Or up until yesterday how he didn't even know she *existed*.

Jake decided to seek an alternate road to return home once he reached the far side of town. He reached the end of Fletcher, turned right and ran down a couple of blocks before turning right on Founder's Way. He had never run on any other road in town besides Fletcher, so this was foreign territory to him. It didn't take him long to understand why.

Overgrown lawns, broken streetlights and every third car on blocks and missing a tire (if not two). The long stretch of asphalt looked every bit as menacing as the Brat Pack. Jake sped up slightly and tried his best to ignore the comments from young men with torn jeans, dirty white T-shirts and cigarettes dangling from the corner of their mouths. *'What are you running from? I'd run too if I were as scrawny as you! Hey, got a cigarette? You DO know you're on our turf, right?'*

Jake looked up and realized he was running straight towards a young, well-dressed woman who appeared to be on her way to either work or church, being it was Sunday and all. He moved over to the right side of the sidewalk to allow her to pass when suddenly one of the thugs wearing torn jeans and a white T-shirt came up behind her, ripped her purse from her shoulder and took off running…

'Like a coward,' Jake thought to himself as he instinctively began chasing after him. It wouldn't take Jake long to catch up with him. Once he did, however, he had a difficult decision: What to do next.

Fortunately instinct took over once again. He snatched the purse out of the thug's hand and kept running all the way to the end of Founder's, took his first two lefts and headed back on Fletcher Street, home of the Blue Harbor Police Department. He ran inside, breathing heavily but still able to relay what had just happened to the uniformed policeman behind the front desk while only stumbling over a couple of words beginning with the sound of a hard 'K,' most notable when he informed them he *'c-c-caught up with the purse snatcher.'*

Jake turned the purse over to the uniformed officer whom immediately reached inside and took out the wallet so he could find the name of its owner. He read silently to himself from the driver's license he discovered slid neatly inside the wallet.

Tina Pittsinger. 119 Founder's Way.

The officer's eyes met Jake's. *'Looks like I need to go for a little drive. Care to ride along?'*

Jake was honored if not a little bit nervous as he thought about Blue Harbor being a small town where everybody seems to know your name.

Being seen in a patrol car is *not* how Jake wanted the good people of Blue Harbor to know the only child of David and Alice Kerslake…and the newest member of the school's cross-country team.

TEN – SUNDAY DINNER

O ne tradition the Kerslake family had maintained for as long as Jake could remember was the Sunday night family dinner. Alice Kerslake firmly believed in it as it was the one time the members of the family could come together and catch up with one another over the events of the past week and discuss what was in store for the week ahead.

So every Sunday night Jake and his parents sat down at the dinner table to a plate of roast beef, homemade mashed potatoes and the vegetable of the week, which usually turned out to be brussel sprouts more often than not. On the really special Sundays when the family had something to celebrate, Jake's mom would prepare one of her special desserts.

Tonight there would be rhubarb pie and vanilla ice cream for dessert. The Kerslakes had something to celebrate.

David Kerslake sat at the head of the table and turned his eyes towards his son. *'Is there something you want to tell us, Jake?'*

Jake was totally oblivious to what his dad had asked. He was too busy thinking about Melissa. Jake slowly lifted his fork from the table and stuck them into the steaming mashed potatoes.

'Jake, we haven't said the blessing yet.' Alice Kerslake reminded him of another family tradition.

After his father said grace, his mom immediately picked up where the conversation had left off earlier. *'So Jake, as your dad was saying; is there something you want to tell us about? Something that happened on Founder's Street, maybe? And by the way: What were you doing on Founder's Street? You know that's not safe!'*

'Oh yeah, that.' Jake wasn't being modest; he simply couldn't quit thinking about the look on Melissa's face as she went about her business as if it were the most important thing in the world. This morning's rescue of a damsel in distress wasn't even a blip on his radar at the moment. *'I saw some guy grab a purse from a lady and I c-c-c-caught up with him and grabbed it back. The police did the rest. C-c-c-could I be excused; I'm not very hungry tonight.'*

Alice Kerslake knew her son well enough to know when he needed some time to himself. This was one of those times.

'Certainly, Jake. I'll warm up some rhubarb pie for you whenever you're ready for it. We've got ice cream, too!'

Jake headed out the front door and made a beeline to the bench in Central Park. Jake needed desperately to talk to JD. He wanted him to be his confidant and mentor… no, he *needed* him to be his confidant and mentor. And now was the time he needed it most.

JD was standing behind the bench tossing peanuts from a brown paper bag to a small congregation of squirrels. Jake could have sworn he heard him calling them by name.

'JD, have you got a minute?'

'Son, I've got nothing but time. What's on your mind? You look like the weight of the world is on your shoulders. How can I help?'

Jake felt an immediate sense of relief—and a little bit of excitement--as he realized this man could indeed be the confidant and mentor he had been hoping for. *'Tell me more about Melissa.'*

JD went on for a solid 45 minutes about how he came to know Melissa and how their friendship had flourished over the years. Melissa came from a broken home—her mother and father had divorced on the day of her 10th birthday—and living alone with her mother she helped make ends meet by working evenings after school and weekends cleaning tables and emptying the trash at the local Happy Burger. With the slightest hint of embarrassment on his face JD admitted Melissa thought of him as a father figure.

Having absorbed every single word JD had said since he arrived, Jake knew exactly why Melissa felt the way she did.

Jake also knew he found what he was looking for. Someone who could help to make him the best runner—not to mention the best *person* he could possibly be.

'*When c-c-c-can we meet again?*' Jake asked, the nervous enthusiasm readily apparent in his voice.

'*How about next Saturday at 6 a.m.? I'll just pencil you in for every Saturday at that time if it's OK with you.*'

Jake had a hard time containing his excitement. '*C-c-c-count on it!*'

As Jake turned to head back home he realized he suddenly had an appetite. '*Hey, c-c-c-care to join me for a piece of rhubarb pie? I c-c-c-can introduce you to my parents.*'

'*I appreciate the offer but I have a few things to take care of around here before I turn in for the night.*'

'*I just realized I don't even know where you live.*'

JD slowly cut his eyes at Jake. '*I believe you do, Jake. I believe you do.*'

ELEVEN – MONDAY BLUES

Some days never turn out as you might expect. For Jake Kerslake, this particular Monday was one of those days.

Jake didn't respond to the alarm clock as he had the past two days. Over the weekend the alarm had the buzz of *'oh-boy-let's-get-this-day-started.'* Today it sounded more like 'oh-lord-let's-get-this-day-over-with.' He was facing a second period history quiz, the 'Monday mystery meat' in the cafeteria and the intensity of Coach Rose, who liked to use Monday's cross-country practice to 'purge the evils' of the previous weekend. Coach Rose knew the propensity for teenage boys to take it easy over the weekends before the season started, gorging on Twinkies and Happy Burgers instead of putting in a couple of miles on the roads to keep the fires burning.

But Coach Rose didn't know the drive and determination of Jake Kerslake. Sure, he knew Jake had the raw physical talent to be one of the best, but he didn't know what was buried deep down inside his heart and soul. As the coach of the Blue Harbor Junior High cross-country team, he knew it was his job to find out.

The school bell signaling the end of second period brought a smile to Jake's face. With the exception of stumbling over the question about General Lee's surrender at Appomattox, he had aced the rest of Mr. Governall's history quiz. Jake left the classroom with one thought in mind: *'NOW let's get this day started!'*

'Hold it right there, Kerslake. I need to talk to you. NOW!'

Jake froze in his tracks. He instantly recognized the booming sound of the voice of the boy who according to school legend is able get a triple serving of Monday mystery meat from sweet Mrs. Tester by simply *glaring* at her behind the counter of food as he stood in the lunch line.

'Was that really you?' Jake wasn't sure what the boy who outweighed him by over 100 pounds was asking.

'I...I'm not really sure what you mean, Tim.' Jake nearly swallowed his tongue getting the sentence out of his mouth. Thank goodness there weren't any words with a hard 'K' sound.

'Yesterday. Founder's Way. The purse snatcher. Was that really you?'

'If you're asking me if I was the one who ran after the goon who grabbed the purse from a young lady, then yes; it was me.' Suddenly Jake was able to breathe again: This was not going to be a hallway version of 'The Pitts' after all.

'I just want you to know that young lady was my sister. My big sister Tina. She means everything to me. She's all I have...'

Jake couldn't believe what he saw next. The Undisputable King of the Brat Pack, TIM FREAKIN' PITTSINGER had tears in his eyes! Jake looked around for witnesses, because he knew no one would believe him if he said TIM FREAKIN' PITTSINGER had tears in his eyes. But by this time most of the students were settled into their third period classrooms. Jake and Tim had this moment all to themselves.

'It really wasn't anything, Tim. I...I mean Mr. Pittsinger.' Jake didn't know why he didn't simply call him 'Tim.' Maybe it's because Tim was two years older. Or maybe it's because Tim was twice his size, or perhaps because leopards can't possibly change their spots and he just might shove him through the wall with the flick of a wrist. Regardless, 'Mr. Pittsinger' felt like the safe choice.

'Pal, don't ever call me anything other than Tim. If there's anything you ever need, I'm your man. I owe you, kid. I owe you BIG!'

With that, Tim Pittsinger turned and walked down the hallway towards the boys' bathroom next to Mr. Governall's classroom. Jake thought he saw Tim take a cigarette out of his back pocket as the door closed behind him.

Jake headed towards his third period class, his adrenaline burning for whatever Coach Rose had in store for him at the end of the day. The fact that the school bully felt like he owed him did nothing to dampen his spirits.

Some days never turn out as you might expect. For Jake Kerslake, this had certainly been one of those days.

TWELVE – TIM PITTSINGER

Tim Pittsinger was known around school for being many things. The bully. The oldest. The biggest. Most of all, the *toughest.*

But there were some things about him that no one knew. The students of Blue Harbor Junior High didn't know Tim Pittsinger, the human being.

Tim lived with his older sister Tina on Flamingo Way. Tina, now a couple of weeks away from her 24th birthday had the responsibility of keeping the family together, something she had done since Jack and Kate Pittsinger were tragically killed seven years earlier in a deadly automobile accident caused by a drunken driver. The people of Blue Harbor called it a miracle that the person responsible for the accident survived the vicious head-on collision, an accident that left 17-year old high school junior Tina Pittsinger responsible for providing for herself and her nine-year old brother after losing their parents.

Over the years Tina did the best she could, working at the Friendly Dollar after school and on weekends while 'Timmy' (Tina was the only person on earth who could get away with calling him by that name) mowed lawns, washed cars and did whatever he could to contribute to the Pittsinger family fund.

With lots of hard work, too many dinners of Raman noodles to count and the love only siblings faced with the loss of both parents can share, the two of them managed to work together to make ends meet. After Tina graduated from Blue Harbor Senior High she was able to find steady employment with the smaller of the two banks in town. The truth of the matter is the manager of the *larger* bank in town once made Tina an offer to work for him at a slightly higher salary (he had heard through the grapevine what a tremendous asset she was) but Tina's sense of loyalty to the manager of the smaller bank kept her where she was. A few days after she politely turned down the offer from the larger bank, Tina was given a respectable raise: Her manager heard through that same grapevine about the larger bank's offer and appreciated her loyalty, something he knew didn't come along very often.

Tim had the same work ethic as Tina, but not the same attitude. While Tina was focused on persevering through the worst storm imaginable—the loss of both parents at an early age and the responsibility of raising her younger brother—Tim's focus was anger: Angry the two most important people in his life were taken away from him at such an early age; angry there was no one to take care of him and his sister; angry because it was seemingly just the two of them against the world. Once Tina graduated from high school and started working full time at the bank, Tim had a lot more time to be alone. Tim didn't use the time constructively; he used it to become even angrier.

Tim soon developed a reputation at Blue Harbor Elementary as the boy who stole your lunch money…the boy who met you at the flagpole after school…the boy the other boys didn't want to be in the bathroom with at the same time because they feared they would have their head shoved in the toilet. You could say that Tim Pittsinger was simply known as *that guy*.

Make no mistake: Tim Pittsinger loved his sister with all his heart. Beyond that, however, he was mad. Mad at the *world*.

What the world didn't know was that inside of his sister's purse—the purse Jake Kerslake chased down and recovered—was all the money in the world the Pittsinger family had to its name. Money for rent, money for groceries and money to pay the rest of the monthly bills. In other words, the money Tina and Tim Pittsinger needed to *survive*.

The good people of Blue Harbor were on the threshold of meeting the *real* Tim Pittsinger. The same one Tina had known all of her life.

Tim Pittsinger; Brother, orphan, human being.

THIRTEEN – GETTING DOWN TO BUSINESS

n his entire career Coach Bill Rose had never witnessed anything like it in 37 years of coaching. 'It,' in this case being the freshman Phenom Jake Kerslake.

On Monday Jake led the team on a 10-mile time trial from start to finish, finishing a full two minutes ahead of a visibly exhausted Eric Shay and five minutes ahead of the third runner. On Tuesday Jake ran six consecutive 800's, each one faster than the one before--a most impressive feat in interval training. Wednesday he ran another 43 seconds faster than Monday for 10 miles, this time a full five minutes ahead of a spent Eric Shay and almost seven minutes ahead of the next best runner the team had to offer. Thursday's timed one mile at the end of practice was a legitimate 'no contest.' Jake was the only one on the team to run it in less than five minutes. As for Friday's casual five-mile run, what Jake did was anything but casual. If the five-mile run were a certified competitive distance at the junior high level, Jake's time would have been within 15 seconds of the school record.

After the team showered and toweled off following Friday's practice, Coach Rose assembled the boys in the locker room. He figured the time was right: The first meet of the season would be at the end of the school day on Tuesday when Blue Harbor would renew its long-time rivalry with nearby South Gate Junior High.

'Great practice this week, men. You've all been very diligent putting in the miles, the time and the effort to perform at your best. Tuesday will be your first opportunity of the season to prove to yourselves it was worth it. As I see it you all have something to be proud of. There's no doubt in my mind that by Tuesday

night the entire county will sit up and take notice of what I've known for a couple of weeks now: That the Blue Harbor Herons have what it takes to be the best team in the county. But first things first: Get some rest this weekend, eat right, drink plenty of water, mind your manners and remember your number one priority right now is your academics. Now get of here and have a great weekend; you've all earned it.'

Coach Rose thought to himself that he hadn't delivered a similar rah-rah speech to one of his teams in over two decades. Then again he never had a team with two talented runners like Jake Kerslake and Eric Shay before, which gave the veteran coach goose bumps simply imagining the possibilities of what the season might have in store for him. Before they could get away he called Jake and Eric into his office for one final word with them.

'You two boys…no, you two MEN are looked up to by everyone on this team. I'm entrusting you both to take ownership of this team—YOUR team. You've both proven to me you've got what it takes to be two of the finest runners in our county. I want you both to prove to me that my gut is right: That your words and actions will guide…no, will DRIVE this team to be the best team it can possibly be. Can I count on you both?'

Eric Shay was the first to speak up. *'We've got your back, coach. Count on it.'*

Several uncomfortably long seconds later the new kid on the block spoke. *'I'll do my best, c-c-c-coach.'*

Coach Rose's questions about Jake Kerslake were beginning to be answered. Jake was indeed a talented runner. Jake was indeed fast. Jake could indeed compete in practice against his peers when there was no serious pressure to excel.

Now the questions Coach Rose had about young Jake Kerslake had been narrowed down to just two:

> *Is Jake the type of person who can help lead this team,*
> *and can he compete when he's needed to run his best?*

In five days he would be getting his first look at Jake Kerslake in the heat of battle.

Five long days and five sleepless nights.

FOURTEEN – VALENTINE'S DAY

Saturday was Valentine's Day. Until today it had no special meaning or significance whatsoever for Jake other than the bouquet of flowers sure to be found in a vase on the dinner table that evening or mom's kiss-at-the-front-door for dad when he got home from work or, if mom was running late her kiss-in-the-living-room from dad.

Jake stopped by the mailbox when he returned home from his early Saturday morning 'talk & run' with JD. He noticed one particular envelope amongst the monthly bills and various sale flyers that was almost certainly a card, probably for mom with an outside chance of being for dad. So it was easy to imagine Jake's surprise when, after handing mom the stack of mail and heading up the stairs to his bedroom his mom called out: *'Jake, there's something in the mail today addressed to you.'*

Jake's eyes immediately were drawn to the return address neatly written in the upper left-hand corner of the envelope in large looping letters with purple ink. It was the house next door: Jessica's house. He couldn't help but notice the slight smell of perfume emanating from the envelope that up until this very moment he had never 'put a name to.' Today there was no question the scent belonged to Jessica, and he surprised even himself how he never really appreciated it until now.

He carefully opened the envelope, nearly perfecting the cut of a letter-opener with the mere use of his index finger. Inside the envelope was a card. On the outside of the card was a picture of a young girl looking out her second-story bedroom window with the words *'Today is the perfect day to tell you how I feel…'*

On the inside of the card was a young boy in his front yard bouncing a soccer ball on his knee with these words: *'But I'm pretty sure you already know. Happy Valentine's Day.'*

Jake asked himself what Jessica could possibly mean? Know *what*, exactly?

Jake headed downstairs for dinner. Alice Kerslake always knew when her son had a question. She sensed now was one of those times.

'Is there anything I can do for you, Jake?'

Jake handed her the card. *'I got this Valentine's Day card from Jessie but I have no idea what it means.'*

Jake's mom looked it over for only a few seconds before she raised her eyes to meet his. Jake couldn't help but notice it was the same look she had on her face the day about a year ago when she came home to a spaghetti dinner prepared by his dad who had taken off early from work to surprise her.

'What is it, mom? I know you know; tell me!'

'Jake, I think Jessica is telling you she has feelings for you. Beyond-friendship feelings.'

'Mom, that's just c-c-c-crazy. I see Jessie every day. We're best friends. We have been...since we were both k-k-k-kids.'

Jake wasn't sure if he was reciting the facts as he knew them...or if he was trying to convince himself there was no way his mom could possibly be right. Then he came to the realization it didn't matter either way, because after giving it a little bit of thought he knew he had feelings for Jessica—those *beyond-friendship* feelings—as well.

Just before sunset on February 14 Jake Kerslake found himself knocking on the front door of the house next door. He wasn't sure what he was going to say when someone answered his half-hearted knock. If it were one of Jessica's parents he would ask if their daughter was home, buying him a couple more seconds to figure out what to say when Jessica stood before him. If it was Jessica, well, Jake hadn't thought that far ahead.

The door slowly creaked open. Jake leaned his head to the left so he could peer around the side of the door to see who was on the other side.

When he saw who it was he said the only thing that he could think of.

'Thanks for the c-c-c-card. Good night!'

Five minutes later Jake was secure in his bedroom, wondering what he would say to his best friend forever the next time he saw her.

FIFTEEN – MONDAY, MONDAY

I don't like Mondays (tell me why) I don't like Mon-days…

Jake couldn't get the song out of his head. His mind was embroiled in a whirlwind of emotions: Anxious about competing in his first cross-country meet the next day; nervous about seeing Jessica for the first time since he left her standing at her front door two days ago, and angry at his parents for playing their Live Aid CD so often that he couldn't get the lyrics of the Boomtown Rats from repeating over and over in his head.

As he made his way towards his first period class, his mind still spinning and his eyes darting from one student to another searching for the long blond hair belonging to the girl he had known virtually all of his life, Jake wasn't paying attention to where he was walking. That is, up until the point he bumped into Tim Pittsinger, the top of Jake's head barely clipping the bottom of the taller boy's chin.

Jake grimaced, fully expecting to be the target of an impromptu round of 'The Pitts' to start the day. *I don't like Mondays…*

So Jake was totally unprepared for what happened next.

'Sorry, kid. I didn't see you coming. I didn't see you running down my street any this weekend; guess you were running around the park. Hey, a couple of us might come out to watch your track meet tomorrow. You OK with that?'

Jake didn't know what to say, other than correcting Tim: *'Cross-c-c-c-country. It's a cross-c-c-c-country meet, not a track meet.'*

'That's what I said, kid. A couple of us might come out to watch your cross-country meet tomorrow.'

The other students within earshot of their conversation stood with their mouths open; they couldn't believe what they had just witnessed, Blue Harbor Junior High's version of David slaying Goliath.

The rest of Jake's day was, in a word FANTASTIC! He aced his math quiz, traded his Monday Mystery Meat for another student's homemade PB&J and even though it was a light practice after school, his legs felt rested and 'springy'—as Coach Rose called it—and was feeling confident about tomorrow's meet. Best of all that darn Boomtown Rats song was finally out of his head.

Yes, his day was fantastic. However, he had no idea what the *night* had in store for him.

SIXTEEN – THE JITTERS

Coach Rose had a word for it: Jitters.

Jake's mom and dad called it something *their* moms and dads had called it: Butterflies in the stomach.

JD called it a tummy tickle.

Whatever anyone may call it everyone is prone to have it at one time or another: That 'fluttery' feeling in your stomach caused by three equal parts of anxiety, apprehension and the unknown.

If anyone had a reason for the case of the jitters on this particular Monday night it was Jake Kerslake. But not for the reason you might expect.

No, Jake Kerslake had a case of the jitters the minute he glanced out the front bay window and saw the silhouette of a young girl—her familiar long blond ponytail bouncing from side to side in the moonlight—quickly approaching his front porch. It was time for Jake to bring closure to his Valentine's Day conversation with one Ms. Jessica Christine Martin.

Then it came: The knock on the front door.

Jake's head was spinning faster than it was before his first period class earlier in the day. *'It's now or never. Do or die. The moment of truth.'* Jake's imagination always had a way of exaggerating things. But don't tell that to Jake because when he opened that front door it was *indeed* now or never... do or die... the moment of truth.

Jake reached for the doorknob with his right hand after wiping a thin layer of perspiration from it on the side of his shirt. As he pulled the door open he noticed the effect Jessica's effervescent smile was having on his case of the jitters: Calming, soothing...almost relaxing.

'I just wanted to wish you luck on your first meet tomorrow. You can be sure I'll be there cheering you on. Go Herons!'

He wasn't expecting her to say those words, quite evident by his almost immediate reply to her: *'I feel the same way, too.'*

Jessica, never the one to be at a loss for words, quickly realized what Jake was referring to. *'Oh, you mean my Valentine's Day card. I was hoping you would like it. No, I meant to say I was hoping you would understand… that you might feel the same way.'*

Jake smiled to himself, hearing the words to another song his parents played over and over on the stereo, this one by Peter Frampton. *'Do you feel like I do?'*

Jessica picked up on his smile immediately. *'Your face says it all, Jake Kerslake.'*

And with that, Jake and Jessica shared their first kiss on the front porch of the Kerslake residence under a full moon on a chilly Monday evening in the dead of winter.

SEVENTEEN – SPRING IN HIS STEP

Jake Kerslake was awake well before his alarm clock sounded at 6 a.m. playing the usual array of classic rock of local radio station WPTC. If there's one thing David Kerslake can say he successfully passed on to this son, it was his love for the songs of the groups he listened to with *his* father growing up: Led Zeppelin, the Doors, Creedence Clearwater Revival and others who ushered in the '70's. One might say classic rock was now in its third generation in the Kerslake household.

But there would be no *Stairway to Heaven* or *Light My Fire* blaring on the radio this morning. Jake hopped out of bed at 5 a.m., turned off the alarm before it had a chance to sound and hopped in the shower. He packed his Herons uniform, ate a bowl of Honey Nut Cheerio's, wrote his mom a note (*'Off to school. Got my first meet after school—hope you can make it!'*), and headed for the park to see what words of wisdom his friend JD would have for him.

JD, perched on the park bench and sipping a cup of hot coffee knew he'd be getting an early morning visit from his young friend. *'You're up awful early this morning. You remind me of me when I was your age. They used to say it was my job to wake the roosters. Funny thing is they weren't far from the truth.'*

'JD, I'll be running in my first c-c-c-cross-c-c-c-country meet this afternoon. Have you got any last-minute advice for me?'

'You've got to believe in yourself. Picture yourself running strong, breathing evenly, holding your form and never losing sight of the fact that you've done your homework. Have confidence in the blood, sweat and tears you've invested to get

to where you are today.' Then suddenly JD's eyes narrowed for one final piece of advice: *'And remember what Coach Rose told you: Run with your head!'*

'Will you be there, JD? Will you be there to see me run?'

'Sorry kid, but I've got a prior engagement this afternoon. I made a promise to someone and I've always been a man to keep his word. A man ain't nothin' if he doesn't keep his word. If it weren't for that I'd be there in a flash.'

'Then I'll be by this evening to tell you all about it. Will you be around? It might be, oh, seven o'clock or so. I'm not sure how late you'll be out tonight.'

'You can find me right here, Jake. You can find me right here.'

And with that, Jake took off running to school with the mental image of himself running strong, breathing evenly and holding his form as he remembered the many miles he had run—and run *hard* since Coach Rose asked him to join the cross-country team…*to be a Heron.*

Jake always thought Tuesdays were the longest day of the week. If any proof was ever needed to support his belief it was today. Most Tuesdays Jake was guilty of sitting in class and watching the clock above the teacher's head. Regardless of which class he was in, Jake was watching the clock. It was just something about Tuesdays. But *this* Tuesday was different: Jake could actually *hear* the clock ticking off the seconds.

Today was not a day for learning a new algebraic equation or cramming for a spelling test. No, today was a day to don the uniform of the Blue Harbor Herons for the very first time and run alongside—and possibly in front of Eric Shay and lead his new team to victory. Jake was literally having a hard time sitting still as the second hand continued to circle the clock, seemingly in slow motion.

Then at 3:30—*at last!*—the final bell of the day sounded. Jake was the first boy on the team in the locker room, the first to change into his uniform and the first to take a seat on the bench to hear the final instructions from Coach Rose. In fact Jake did all of this before any of the other boys on the team had opened the combination lock on their gym lockers.

Once the eight fastest boys in Blue Harbor Junior High were assembled, Coach Rose didn't waste any time. *I'm proud of you, men. You've worked hard, you've made sacrifices and you've committed yourselves to being the best runners you can possibly be. Today is the first day you have the opportunity to demonstrate that it was all worth it. Let's do this, Herons. LET'S DO THIS!'*

And with those words eight inspired young men—all wearing the school colors of orange and blue —practically flew out of the locker room.

And to no one's surprise Jake Kerslake was the first one out the locker room door.

EIGHTEEN – THE HERON'S LAP

T he Blue Harbor Junior High cross-country course consisted of a 1.55-mile loop through the forest surrounding its modest campus consisting of an administrative complex/auditorium/cafeteria, three difficult-to-distinguish-one-from-another red brick buildings—all with eight equally difficult to distinguish classrooms--and an athletic facility that rivaled that of nearby Blue Harbor Senior High. All of the fields for the school's major team sports—football, baseball and soccer were always kept in immaculate condition, whether the particular sport was in season or not. There was a gymnasium for the basketball and volleyball teams and of course a rubberized 400-meter track and the highly respected path through the trees taken by many a runner over the years that was better known as the 'Heron's Lap.'

This was going to be Jake's first time running the Heron's Lap although he had walked the loop several times during lunch period in eighth grade, his alternative to eating whatever was being served in the cafeteria whenever Ms. Grumby was in charge of preparing the meal. According to Jake, Ms. Grumby was the only person in the world who could make a fish filet taste like chopped liver, something he swore he would never eat after his mom served it for dinner when Jake was seven years old. To this day Jake still gags whenever he thinks of chopped liver, which if it weren't for the days Ms. Grumby made her infamous fish filets would be never.

The first meet of the season was a five-kilometer race, meaning the teams would have to run the Heron's Lap twice for a total of 3.1 miles. Jake made a mental note to ask Coach Rose why they don't simply run an even three miles since kilometers aren't used for measuring anything else.

51

Cedar River is 31 miles away from Blue Harbor; Jake never heard anyone refer to it as 50 kilometers. Why should running be any different? Then again, how much further than three miles is three-point one miles? Maybe another 170 yards or so? *Piece of cake!*

As the meet officials called the runners to the starting line near the south end zone of the football field, Jake wondered why he had never actually run the Heron's Lap before today. After all, every team practice had been run on asphalt. Jake had heard rumors that Coach Rose had a philosophy that those who really want to be the best will take it upon themselves to run the Heron's Lap without being asked to do so. Jake was angry at himself for dropping the ball on this one and for the first time thought he had a glimpse into what Coach Rose meant about him running with his head.

The race began with very little fanfare. Runners from three schools—24 in all—lined up behind a line of white chalk in the green grass in the shadows of the goal posts on the south end of Heron Field. The starter's command was short and to the point: *'Runners to your marks...GO!'* And with that they were off. Seconds later one runner after another disappeared into the woods. All of them would return within 10 minutes to begin their second and final loop.

The first runner to emerge out of the other side of the woods was wearing the orange and blue of Blue Harbor Junior High. So was the second, fifth and sixth runner. The official race clock displayed '8:23' as Jake Kerslake finished his first loop, a full 15 yards in front of teammate Eric Shay. Whereas the expression on Eric's face was one of confidence, the one on Jake's was one of uncertainty. However none of that kept Alice Kerslake and Jessica Martin from screaming hysterically as Jake disappeared into the woods for the second time. Coach Rose silently mouthed the word 'focus' as he attacked the clipboard in his left hand with the pencil he had in his right. Next to the name 'Jake Kerslake' he simply wrote the word he had on his lips seconds earlier. Coach Rose knew two things were about to happen: Eric Shay would be the first one across the finish line, and Jake Kerslake would come to the conclusion he still had a lot to learn.

NINETEEN – LEARNING CURVE

'It was horrible, JD. Everyone was there: Jessica, my mom, half of the students in ninth grade. I think I even saw Tim Pittsinger standing under the bleachers at one time—I can't remember if it was before the race or during the race. Heck, it might have even been after. I was leading the race for the better part of 15 minutes and then, and then...'

JD sipped on his ever-present cup of coffee and noticed how he could see every word Jake was saying in the cold and damp winter air. 'So things didn't go as planned, eh?'

Jake explained—more so with his hands than with his words—how he led the race for two-and-three-quarter miles when suddenly he lost control not only of his legs but of his ability to generate coherent thoughts as well. 'I was ahead of Eric Shay and everyone else by a good 30 yards when suddenly my legs started to feel like they were made of rubber and the only thing on my mind was Lord-please-don't-let-me-fall-flat-on-my-face.'

'Welcome to the Learning Curve, young warrior. Consider today as your first lesson.' JD took another sip, followed by this: 'Ahhh...it doesn't get much better than this!'

'JD, you don't understand! I failed today. I let my team down. I let my mom down. I let Jessica down. I let C-c-c-coach Rose down. I let YOU down...'

Jake's voice trailed off to little more than a whisper. 'I let myself down.'

JD's eyes widened as the slightest hint of a smile appeared on his face. 'What are you doing this Saturday? If you're free I think I might be able to help.'

Those were the words Jake wanted to hear...needed to hear. 'Sounds great. About seven, then?'

'Make it six.'

53

TWENTY – A LITTLE HELP FROM HIS FRIENDS

The strangest thing happened during the rest of the week. The entire school—the students, the faculty, the janitor, even mean ole' Ms. Grundy were nothing but sources of encouragement and appreciation following Jake's cross-country debut. In Jake's mind he finished in a disappointing ninth place; in everyone else's mind he represented the essence of bravery, a lithe 94-pound boy willing to take on the challenges of the most physically-demanding sport of all, long distance running.

Tim Pittsinger, the leader of the infamous Brat Pack was arguably the most supportive one of all, even offering to work with Jake in the weight room on the days the meals in the school cafeteria weren't particularly appetizing. Jake said Tim could 'count him in' on Mystery Meat Mondays and any other day Ms. Grundy was in charge of preparing lunch. Tim and Jake were quickly becoming friends—some would say even *good* friends— and the entire student body began keeping a mental stick tally of how many days it had been since the last episode of 'The Pitts' (16 and counting).

Two days after practice--Wednesday and Friday--Coach Rose asked Jake to step into his office after the team finished its workout. The veteran coach explained what separates the great runners from the good runners. *'Most of the better runners are blessed with a comparable amount of physical talent. What makes the better runners the best is what goes on between their ears. It's important to think…to FOCUS every step of the way. Is this the best pace for me to be running at this point in the race? Am I running all of the tangents? Am I speeding up—or slowing down if necessary at the right time?*

How do my legs feel? Am I drinking enough water? How is my breathing—nice and steady or am I sucking for air? Are my shoulders back, chin held high? It never stops…at least not until you cross that finish line. Make sense?' Yes, Coach Rose made a lot of sense. Jake nodded his head in agreement so much in those two sessions with his coach that he had a mental image of himself as a bobble head doll wearing an orange and blue running uniform.

Thursday was memorable for the simple fact that Jake and Jessica went out on their very first date. The date was made official when Jake asked the girl next door if she would like to go for a milk shake after dinner at Happy Burger. Once she agreed they walked hand-in-hand up until the moment they were seated next to one another on barstools at the counter. Jake, feeling better about himself, about his life, about *everything* than he had since the day he brought home a 'straight A' report card in fourth grade made it a point to strike up a conversation with Melissa, who happened to be working that night. Once they were formerly introduced, Jessica and Melissa struck up a conversation that if Jake didn't know any better would have led one to believe they were long-lost friends who hadn't seen one another in years.

Cross-country practices were also going well. The next meet wouldn't be until the following Tuesday, and Jake was counting on the adrenaline he was feeling from everyone's support and encouragement, the hard workouts he was doing and whatever JD had in store for him Saturday to make this next meet a good one. One that he and everyone else—his teammates, his parents, his girlfriend, his coach—would be proud of.

Most of all he wanted to make his new friend in the park proud.

TWENTY-ONE – SATURDAY IN THE PARK

Jake had every intention of showing up at the bench in Central Park a good 15 minutes earlier than 6:00 a.m. on Saturday morning because for once—*just once* he wanted to be a step ahead of JD. Jake noticed how JD had a knack for being out in front of things, whether it be predetermined times for the two of them to meet, what was on Jake's mind on any given day or how Jake's day had gone (in the classroom, at cross-country practice, at home—it made no difference). Today Jake intended to beat JD at his own game by showing up at their chosen meeting spot first.

Jake glanced at his watch as he saw the top of the lamppost that illuminated the park bench located directly beneath it. The watch read '5:39.' Jake felt good about his chances of beating JD to the punch... until his eyes followed the lamppost from top to bottom where he saw JD, with his all-too-familiar hot cup of coffee perched firmly between his hands as he sat quietly on the bench waiting for his young friend to arrive.

'I hope you're wearing your walking shoes today. I've got some people I want you to meet and we're going to have to cover some real estate by foot to do it. You in?'

'Looking forward to it, JD. Let's roll.'

And just like that they were off to begin the next chapter in *The Book of Life* authored by one Jefferson Saine Douglas.

The two walked side-by-side in the brisk, chilling February wind on the sidewalk encircling the park. It seemed like the walk took forever which, based on what Jake observed is about how long it took JD to finish drinking his morning cup of coffee. By the time JD abruptly stopped and announced '*here we are*' Jake couldn't believe the coffee remaining in his cup could possibly still be the slightest bit warm on a bitterly cold day like today.

'Where are we, exactly?' It seemed odd—even to Jake—that for a route he had run many, many times he had never noticed anything but the asphalt immediately in front of him. He couldn't help but notice the irony of Coach Rose's advice of covering the paths as fast as you could, or something like that. It seems Jake had been doing just that since the first time he wore a pair of high tops and took off running for no particular reason other than to see if he could.

Jake caught a glimpse of a small white building in desperate need of repair at precisely the same time JD raised his arm and pointed to the exact same spot.

'Where we should be,' JD replied. Jake couldn't help but notice the smile on JD's face revealed quite a bit of gold in the corners of his mouth. *'I want you to meet a very, very good friend of mine. I believe you'll like her.'*

Jake and JD crossed the street. JD was well in front of his young companion, so much that the thought of the phrase 'age before beauty' brought a smile to Jake's face. JD pulled open the door—a door that didn't appear to have any intention of opening until JD tugged on it with a right hand finally free of the cup of coffee that had been glued to it for the past half hour or more.

'Good morning, my brothers and sisters!' The excitement in JD's voice reminded Jake of Christmas mornings past. *'Where might I find the lovely Miss B?'*

Jake heard a click-click-click sound approaching from the hallway to his left. A young boy—probably an inch or two shy of four feet tall—was using his cane to do the work his eyes should have been doing. *'She's out with Mikey and the others, but she should be back soon.'* The boy's name was Dylan, and from the day he was born he had never been blessed with the gift of sight.

'You tell Miss B I was here and if she's in the park later today to look me up. I have someone I'd like her to meet.' It was apparent to Jake that Dylan and JD knew one another.

'You know I will, Mister JD.'

Jake was right: Dylan and JD *did* know one another.

TWENTY-TWO – MISS B

'Who is Miss B?' Jake could hardly contain his curiosity as he paced step-for-step alongside JD on their brisker-than-ever walk back to the park. Their conversation was so energized neither one of them noticed how fast they were walking nor the reason why. If questioned about it JD might think it was Jake who was walking at a frantic pace, unable to contain his enthusiasm and excitement about the mysterious Miss B. Jake, however might have pointed the finger at JD, arguing he was moving along faster than normal to generate enough body heat to fight off the chills of the freezing morning temperatures. Regardless of the reason, Jake's rat-a-tat questioning barely afforded JD the time to slide in an answer or two.

'How do you know Miss B? What does the letter 'B' stand for, or is it actually 'Bee' with two B's?' Is she related to you? Does she work at the building we were just in? That boy said she was out with Mikey and the boys. Who are Mikey and the boys?'

Once Jake stopped long enough to catch his breath, JD calmly asked for his permission to answer. Slightly embarrassed, Jake dropped his chin to his chest and whispered. *'Yes. That is, if you don't mind.'*

'Why I don't mind one bit,' JD replied. *'I first met Sandy Bowers—Miss B to most everyone in Blue Harbor—on the day she was born. I was good friends with her grandfather and his wife at the time Sandy's momma Christine, whom everyone called Mrs. B—gave birth to Sandy. Let me tell you: Sandy was a fireball from the start. Most infants walk around 12 months—Sandy was doing it in six and never looked back. She learned to ride a bike without ever using training wheels. She loved the outdoors; still does, as a matter of fact. She spends*

59

a lot of time on the weekend riding her baby blue beachcomber all over this very park. It wouldn't surprise me one bit if we don't bump into her at some point.'

'She sounds like a neat lady, JD. But what's a beach c-c-c-comber?' It was obvious JD had Jake's full attention.

'I guess I'm showing my years a bit. It's an old fashioned bicycle designed for use on the beach. It has only one speed and has really big and fat tires, pretty much unlike any bike you've ever seen. And yes, she is a very special young lady…which you are about to find out for yourself.'

Jake turned around suddenly to discover the source of the *ring-ring-ring* coming from behind him. He caught a glimpse of a fender the color of a robin's egg and a smile that instantly made him think of the song by Bad English his mom and dad played at night once they mistakenly thought Jake was asleep:

When I see you smile, I see a ray of light…

'Hi JD! It sure is a wonderful morning to be outside, isn't it? Have you been by the house this morning? I know the kids were looking forward to seeing you.'

Although they had never formally met, this woman's radiant smile, sparkling personality and last but not least baby blue beachcomber—this had to be what JD was talking about because he'd never seen a bike like it before—left no doubt in Jake's mind that this energetic young lady had to be Sandy, the mysterious Miss B.

'We stopped by but decided to come to the park hoping to run into you. This must be our lucky day.' Jake took silent note of how JD suddenly seemed more relaxed, comfortable and at peace with the world once Miss B showed up. *'I especially wanted you to meet my new friend Jake. One day Jake is going to be remembered as the fastest runner in the history of Blue Harbor High— yep, even faster than your dear grandfather.'*

'Pleased to meet you, soon to be the fastest runner in school history!' Charm and flattery had always been two of Miss B's strongest assets.

Jake stumbled over his reply. *'JD c-c-c-can exaggerate sometimes, Miss B.'* Sandy could tell the slight stutter was a source of embarrassment for Jake.

'I once knew a young lady who had a difficult time pronouncing almost any word that began with a consonant. Through her time with us at Best Foot Forward she was able to overcome it and is now an assistant professor at a small

university upstate. And she teaches public speaking, of all things! And feel free to call me Sandy.' She now had Jake's full attention.

Jake was now curious. *'What is Best Foot Forward?'* He had heard the phrase from JD on more than one occasion and considered it nothing more than a coincidence that Sandy would use it as well. He also thought to himself that Sandy Bowers appeared larger than life and he didn't feel comfortable calling her by her first name. Not yet, anyway. After all, *they just met!*

'Best Foot Forward is the organization I work for out of the building you and JD visited earlier this morning. My staff and I work with those with special needs—mentally and physically challenged children and young adults, helping them prepare for life once they complete their formal education. Of course we all know we never stop learning, but after graduation things change…LIFE changes and we want our clients to be ready to take their next step in life. Our name—Best Foot Forward comes from a phrase JD and my grandfather adopted when they were running for Blue Harbor High School a while back.'

So many thoughts were swirling around in Jake's mind it was impossible for him to focus on any one thing. He found Miss B absolutely fascinating…JD's previous life as a runner surprising…the purpose of Best Foot Forward inspirational. Jake could literally feel the blood pulsating through his body. He had never felt so alive in his life, yet he discovered he was only capable of uttering a single word out loud:

'Wow.'

TWENTY-THREE — BEST FOOT FORWARD

'I *can tell by the look on your face you're a little surprised to discover your friend JD used to be quite the runner!'* That was another of Miss B's special qualities: The ability to read people. *'JD and my grandfather were practically inseparable when they were your age. They went everywhere together, and I do mean everywhere. To get wherever it was they wanted to go they had to do it on foot, and it didn't take them long to realize they could get there a lot faster if they ran. So that's what they did. They ran; every day and everywhere. I recall them telling me they once ran all the way to Cedar River. That's an hour away BY CAR! By the time JD and my grandfather started high school they were well known by everyone in Blue Harbor. By the time they were seniors they were the top two high school runners in the entire state. They coined the phrase 'best foot forward' because that was their philosophy: To always give their absolute best into everything they did.'*

'So that's where you got the name for your organization?' Jake was hanging onto every word she spoke and he couldn't wait to hear more.

'It's true that's where the name came from, but it didn't come from me. JD and my grandfather started this organization not long after they graduated from high school. They desperately wanted to give something back to the community that had taken so much pride in promoting them as ambassadors of Blue Harbor.' Jake couldn't help but notice the sparkle in her eyes as she spoke. He silently hoped that one day he would have something to be as proud of as Miss B was of Best Foot Forward and the two men responsible for creating it.

Jake was equally impressed by his friend JD's modesty. He wondered if JD would have ever said anything about establishing Best Foot Forward had Miss B never mentioned it. Jake wondered what other secrets JD had been keeping from him during their short friendship. He optimistically thought to himself that one day he would find the courage to ask. Of course, that day would never come: Jake was never the type of person who could pry into someone else's affairs.

'Well, I think I should be heading back. Why don't you stop by one day and I'll give you a tour and introduce you to some of the gang? It would be my pleasure.' It was clear to Jake that her invitation was sincere.

'O-K-K-K...' Jake was amazed that today his stutter didn't cause him the slightest bit of embarrassment. *'I sure will!'*

As Miss B rode off on her beachcomber Jake told JD he never remembered him saying so little. In fact he couldn't remember JD ever going this long without speaking. It was obvious to Jake that Miss B—Sandy—was someone very special to JD. He too seemed to be hanging on her every word, in spite of the fact he had probably heard them many times before.

It wouldn't be long before Jake would realize she had that effect on virtually everyone she met.

TWENTY-FOUR – WHY NOT ME?

I t wasn't easy for Jake to tell JD he was going to have to pass on their regular Saturday morning pow-wow. But the second he said he was going to spend the day with Miss B and the children at Best Foot Forward, Jake could tell by the look on his face that he had JD's full support.

Jake arrived at the one-story brick building—Miss B's pride and joy—and noticed a sign in the front yard he hadn't noticed before. *'Why Not Me?'* was carved ever-so-neatly into a four-foot piece of oak sitting proudly beneath the window of the office of 'Sandy Bowers, BFF Executive Director' as the much smaller piece of oak on her office door proclaimed. Jake couldn't help but notice the letters on both signs appeared to have been carved by the same pair of hands.

Miss B met Jake at the front door before he even had a chance to ring the doorbell. *'Good morning, young Mr. Kerslake. I just want to say that I'm thrilled you're spending your Saturday morning with our extended family. The kids feel the same way.'*

Jake quickly glanced at the area immediately behind Miss B. He couldn't believe that 11 or 12 children had gathered in the small foyer he could have sworn was vacant no less than 15 seconds earlier. *'HI JAKE!'* the kids shouted out in unison. Jake returned the salutation and the next thing he knew every single child was shouting out their names at the same time as if Jake had a super power that enabled him to remember a dozen names thrown upon him at once. Jake responded with *'Hi back!'* hoping it would buy him some time to learn everyone's name throughout the course of the morning. Several hours later he would discover his plan worked out perfectly. So perfectly that he would have 12 new acquaintances he would know as friends before the day was over.

The first face Jake was drawn to was a familiar one: Melissa, Jake's classmate from Oak Harbor Lane. *'What brings you to our little oasis, Jake?'* Jake couldn't help but notice how melodic her voice sounded. *'Miss B invited me to spend the day with the k-k-k-kids,'* he replied.

'Gee Jake, I never knew you stuttered. At one time I stuttered myself—I had a lot of trouble with words starting with the letter 'f.' That's why I'm in charge of clean up at Happy Burger; at first I worked the register but I had a lot of trouble asking the customers if they wanted fries with their order.'

Jake couldn't help but notice the wry smile on Melissa's face. *'Are you being serious?'*

'Only about the stuttering, Jake. I really did have a problem with words starting with an 'f,' but being here with Miss B and the others has had a huge impact on my life. I got rid of the stutter and learned to appreciate who I am and what I have to offer. I'm just a totally different person; a better person. I enjoy my life and I enjoy being me. I never would have suspected in a million years I could ever say something like that. This place means the world to me.' Jake noticed the look on Melissa's face as she was speaking; it confirmed every single word she said.

'This place must be something special,' Jake replied. A slight smile crossed his face as he realized that what he just said would likely be the frontrunner for Understatement of the Year, if an award for such a thing were given.

Just about that time two boys—maybe eight or nine years old—ran up to Jake and wrapped their tiny arms around his waist. *'I'm Mikey,'* said the shorter of the two. *'I'm Dylan,'* said the other. Jake instantly recognized Mikey had Down Syndrome because two of the bag boys he knew who worked at Hungry Lion every Monday and Wednesday afternoons had the same disability. As for Dylan, Jake wouldn't have suspected anything out of the ordinary if it wasn't for the fact Dylan walked with a cane…and asked Jake if he would bend down so he could touch his face.

'Sure, Dylan.' He barely got the words out before Dylan had his hands on either side of Jake's face. Dylan said *'I can tell you're a very nice man.'* Jake couldn't decide if he was more surprised by Dylan's analysis or the fact he referred to him as a 'man;' after all he was only 14 and had never so much

as shaved, let alone done anything to make him a man. *'Thanks?'* was the only reply he could muster.

'How long have you two been coming to BFF?' Jake was honestly interested in the answer, as he couldn't get over how friendly and outgoing everyone seemed to be.

'Ever since we learned to walk,' they replied in unison. Mikey went on to add: *'This place makes us feel proud of who we are'* which led to Dylan shouting out *'and special!'*

Jake stayed until he could sense his mom back home setting the dinner table. As Jake was about to leave he looked to Mikey and asked the meaning behind the sign out front asking 'Why Not Me?'

Mikey, sounding 10 years more mature than his age replied *'Many people in our shoes would ask themselves 'why me?'* He explained. *'Here at BFF we prefer to say why NOT me? Who better to deal with our challenges than each and every one of us here? We're all proud of whom we are, and as Miss B tells us over and over again, we make a difference; we matter.'*

Jake rubbed Mikey on the head with his left hand as he headed out the door. He used his right hand to wipe a tear from the corner of his eye.

TWENTY-FIVE – BIRTH OF A RUNNER

Monday's practice went well; just what Jake needed to boost his confidence heading into Tuesday's meet with the runners from Radford and Halsey. Coach Rose saw it in Jake's face as he was putting on his uniform in the locker room 30 minutes before the start of the five-kilometer race. *'This is going to be Jake's breakout moment, I just know it!'* It was a comforting thought that brought a huge smile across his normally emotionless face.

Less than an hour later another smile—this one larger than the one before—could be seen on the veteran coach's face. For today Jake Kerslake ran a race for the ages, in and of itself a strange way to describe it since the young man was still only 14 years old. But if you were looking to find a textbook demonstration of how to run three miles, today was the day. Jake ran most of the first two miles completely within himself—a fancy way of saying he ran a pace that felt comfortable to him—and then turned it up a couple of notches for the remaining mile or so until he crossed the finish line, his nearest competitor a good 50 yards behind. What really caught Coach Rose's attention was the look on Jake's face as he appeared to get stronger and stronger as the race went on. He couldn't quite put his finger on the look: *Confidence? Arrogance? Faith? Conviction?* He made a mental note to ask Jake what was going through his mind during those 16 minutes (and a couple of seconds) the next day at practice. For now he just wanted to savor the moment; a moment he knew was coming ever since the day he saw Jake running from the so called 'Brat Pack' from the seat of his bicycle.

Yes, he wanted to savor the moment: It wasn't every day Bill Rose got to witness a defining moment such as this.

The birth of a runner.

TWENTY-SIX — MIKEY

T he first words out of Coach Rose's mouth as his runners entered the locker room for Wednesday's practice were directed at young Jake Kerslake, less than 24 hours removed from one of the finest races the veteran coach had ever seen. *'I don't know what you had for breakfast yesterday but I suggest you share that menu with your teammates because next week we're running against last year's county champs and we're going to need everything we've got!'*

Every eye in the locker room was fixated on the smile slowly developing on the face of yesterday's victor. *'Just trying to put my best foot forward, c-c-c-coach.'* Coach Rose could tell by the look on Jake's face there was more to the story, but for now he seemed satisfied to leave it at that.

Jake not only was the fastest runner three times around the Heron's Lap, he was also the fastest to shower, dress and exit the locker room after practice. It wasn't that he needed to rush home because he had a lot of homework or his mother was making his favorite meal (meat loaf, mashed potatoes and lima beans), but rather because he was in a hurry to spend some time with his new friend Mikey. After Tuesday's victory running against Radford and Halsey and celebratory dinner of—what else?—meat loaf, mashed potatoes and lima beans Jake called Miss B on the telephone. Their conversation went like this:

Jake: *'Hi Miss B, it's me Jake. Would it be O-k-k-k-k if I c-c-c-came by after practice tomorrow and spent some time with Mikey?'*

Miss B: *'Sure thing, Jake. Mikey will love it! How did you do in today's meet, by the way?'*

Jake: *'O-k-k-k-k. See you tomorrow. Thanks, Miss B!'*

One can only imagine Sandy Bowers' surprise when she read in Saturday's edition of the *Harbor Press* that Jake's run in Tuesday's meet ranked as one of the top five fastest races in county history. The article pointed out that Jake was the only freshman amongst those top five and that his potential hadn't yet been reached; *'not by a longshot'* is how the writer phrased it. Sandy thought of Jake calling his run 'OK' and how much it reminded her of the time one of the youngsters at Best Foot Forward referred to the writings of William Shakespeare, arguably one of the finest writers of all time as *'not too shabby.'*

As if the four-and-a-half mile workout after school wasn't enough, Jake ran the entire three-mile route to Best Foot Forward at a speed Coach Rose would have had a hard time keeping up with on his trusty bicycle. He ran to the front door, knocked five times (tap, tap…tap, tap, tap) and within seconds Mikey pulled the front door open with a smile on his face that made Jake think of a phrase his father used to describe rather large things; *'as wide as the Pacific.'*

'HI JAKE IT'S GREAT TO SEE YOU WHAT ARE WE GOING TO DO TODAY?' Mikey could barely contain his excitement as he rushed outside, leaving the door wide open and for Jake to close.

'I thought we could go for a walk around the park. Pretty much the same route JD and I take every Saturday morning. That is, every Saturday morning we don't make a detour and swing by Best Foot Forward which, now that I've met you, Dylan, Melissa, Miss B and the others won't be very often.' Jake noticed the smile on Mikey's face seemed even wider than it was earlier before he started to wonder if that was even possible.

But that's what Jake had come to realize with the good folks at Best Foot Forward: With just the right combination of confidence, faith and conviction, anything is possible.

The instant Jake and Mikey crossed the street and entered the park, Mikey took control. *'Let's go this way, Jake. There's so much I want to show you. There's so much I want to tell you. There's just…SO MUCH!'* Jake had no idea what Mikey had in store for him, but it didn't matter: This had the possibility of being ONE GREAT AFTERNOON!

'Do you like plants, Jake? I do. I love studying plants. Do you know that bamboo can grow 35 inches in a single day? Do you know Snapdragon flowers resemble a dragon, and if you squeeze the sides the dragon's mouth will open and close? Do you know trees are the longest living organisms on earth and the tallest ones are Redwoods? Do you know there are more than 80,000 species of edible plants on earth? Edible means you can eat them, you know.'

If it weren't for the enthusiasm in Mikey's voice and the excitement written all over his face, Jake might have mistaken this walk in the park for his fourth period science class. No, this afternoon was all about enjoying the companionship of a young boy who had both eyes wide open, enjoyed the beauty of the world around him and made the most of every single moment he had.

Today Mikey was not only teaching Jake about nature and the world around him; he was also teaching him about life.

It was a day Jake would never forget as it opened up his eyes to so many things he never thought about before.

At the top of his list: Doing whatever it takes to put his best foot forward in everything he does.

TWENTY-SEVEN – DYLAN

Jake had such a good time spending the afternoon with Mikey he called Miss B later that same night to ask if he could spend some time with Dylan the following day. Miss B was quick to give her permission (although 'blessing' might be a more appropriate word).

After practice the next day Jake headed straight to Best Foot Forward, where he was greeted at the front door with the same enthusiasm as the day before. Dylan instantly recognized Jake; not by sight but by the sound of his voice when Jake said *'missed you yesterday, Dylan.'* This exchange brought smiles to both of their faces, causing Jake to wonder if Dylan had ever been witness to an actual smile before. During the course of the afternoon Jake would learn many, many things about nature (one of Dylan's favorite subjects, no doubt inspired by his friend Mikey), about the wonderful things Best Foot Forward does and the fact that Dylan was blind from birth, answering the question as to whether or not he had actually seen a smile before.

Once the pleasantries were out of the way, Dylan simply said to Jake *'I'm ready if you are. Now follow me!'* On that note Dylan's walking cane began 'tap-tap-tapping' on the front walkway, took a hard right on the sidewalk running parallel to the street which they followed for almost half a mile before Dylan abruptly stopped at a pedestrian walkway and waited for the light to change—which Dylan could tell by the 'tweeting' sound at the intersection indicating it was safe to cross the road and head into the park.

As they made their way through the park—with Dylan CLEARLY being the one in control—Jake was being inundated with so much information he thought he was in a biology class for honors students.

'Smell that? Those are hydrangeas. Do you know there are more than 70 species of them?' 'Smell that? Those are dandelions. They open in the morning and close in the evening—like they're going to sleep or something. Weird, huh?' 'Smell that? Daffodils. My dad gave my mom a bouquet of them for their 10th wedding anniversary.'

Jake managed to get a few words in edgewise, if only to give his brain a rest from all this knowledge being thrown in its direction. *'Smell that? C-c-c-cocker Spaniel.'* The intended levity apparently escaped Dylan because he immediately picked up where he left off. *'Smell that? Gardenias. They're usually white or pale yellow, but I bet those are closer to brown. They turn that color if water touches them and since it rained earlier this afternoon...'*

As the two of them were getting ready to exit the park, Jake asked Dylan how he knew so much about flowers. *'Mikey taught me a lot, but a lot I learned from talking to people in the park. I probably learned the most from JD, though. The man is a GEE-NEE-USSS! One thing JD told me a long time ago that I'll remember all my life is this: Be sure to stop and smell the roses. So that's exactly what I do except I do it for all of the flowers, not just the roses. Roses, by the way are a great source of Vitamin C. Not many people know that, but they are.'*

Jake was amazed. Amazed at Dylan's knowledge of flowers, especially at such a young age. Amazed at Dylan's zest for life. Amazed at Dylan's amazing outlook of the world around him when the only thing he had ever seen in his entire life was darkness.

'Best Foot Forward, Miss B and her kids, JD,' he thought to himself, *'are amazing.'* Jake could sense a huge smile break out across his face and a look of awareness—no, 'enlightenment' might be a better word—in his eyes. Feeling a little embarrassed about it Jake was sort of relieved young Dylan wasn't able to see the look on his face. Then he felt bad about having that thought.

'I can tell your imagination is running wild, Jake.' Dylan nailed it.

Jake thought that Dylan probably saw more in his short time on earth being blind than most people with perfectly good vision see in a lifetime. Then he realized it was more than just a thought; it was a fact.

TWENTY-EIGHT — EVERYTHING'S COMING UP ROSES

Things were going quite well for young Jake Kerslake.

Friday's meet with Parkview and Sandstone turned into a two-man race between Jake and Eric Shay as they played a high-speed game of leap frog for three miles before running the last couple hundred yards together and finishing in a dead heat for first place. While the two never had any notable interactions or conversations prior to the meet, they bonded more in those grueling 16 minutes than some people do in a lifetime.

Saturday morning with JD was memorable in the sense that—for once, anyway—Jake did most of the talking. He told JD he was starting to understand 'what running is all about,' in his words and how well the week's two meets went. Jake was so excited he failed to mention that he finished first in both of them (albeit the second one ended in a photo-finish tie), a fact JD may never have known had he not asked. Jake raved about his relationship with Miss B and his afternoons with Mikey and Dylan; JD smiled and nodded the entire time even though he had known Mikey and Dylan since they were preschoolers and practically knew what Jake was going to say before he had a chance to say it. Yes, today JD's job was to simply listen and enjoy the excitement and enthusiasm in his young protégé.

Saturday afternoon he stopped in at Best Foot Forward to thank Miss B for the opportunity to get to know Mikey and Dylan. As Jake stepped into her office he noticed a wealth of hand-made posters in nice barn wood frames on all four walls. The artwork was simple yet elegant in the sense that it was done by the hands of the youngsters who spent most of their afternoons and weekends there. Most telling of all were the phrases, as they painted an even clearer picture of the philosophy and teachings of Sandy Bowers and the staff at Best Foot Forward:

Stop and Smell the Roses

WE MATTER!

Why Not Me?

FAITH In Every Child

Jake smiled to himself as his eyes bounced from one frame to another. *'Miss B, I'd love it if you and some of the k-k-k-kids c-c-c-could c-c-c-come to my meet on Tuesday. C-c-c-can you…I mean they c-c-c-come?'* With a gentle smile and a wink in her eye, she replied: *'We'll be honored, Jake.' Count on us being there.'*

Saturday night Jake took Jessica out for dinner at the Happy Burger and a movie afterward. The movie, of course, was the latest 'creature feature.' Jake loved it and for Jake's sake, Jessica pretended she loved it as well. Melissa was working Saturday night, but it just so happened that her 15-minute break at 9 p.m. was about the time Jake and Melissa's dinner was brought to their table so the three of them dined together, talking and laughing as if they were lifelong friends.

Sunday morning Jake went out for a long run of 10 (or maybe 13 miles—time passed by so quickly it made it difficult to tell for certain) with his teammate and new friend Eric Shay. Their route took them by Tim Pittsinger's house and Jake thought he was seeing things when he saw Tim tossing a bowling ball in the yard—actually more sand and dirt than 'yard'—on the side of the house. Jake noticed a tiny hand waving from one of the windows. It belonged to Tim's sister Tina, who was thinking to herself as Jake ran by: *'If it weren't for that brave, young boy Tim and I might not be living here right now.'*

Sunday afternoon allowed Jake to catch up on some things. First up: An hour on homework. Next: Several hours to catch up on a couple of *Creature Features* he recorded off of Channel 6 earlier in the week.

Sunday evening—for the second time this week—Jake enjoyed a home cooked meal of meat loaf, mashed potatoes and lima beans. His parents bombarded him with questions about his week and for once, Jake had plenty to say.

As he climbed into bed to rest up for another week on the run, Jake gave his nightly prayer some thought before settling on this:

Dear Lord,
Thank you. Just thank you.
Amen.

Yes, things were going quite well for young Jake Kerslake.

Before nodding off for the night he even started to sing, paraphrasing a song he heard his mother sing in the kitchen on more than one occasion:

'Nothing's Gonna Stop Me Now.'

TWENTY-NINE — SEEING IS BELIEVING

Monday afternoon as the Blue Harbor Herons were running their usual beginning-of-the-week workout of three slow and easy circuits of Heron's Lap, Jake noticed out of the corner of his eye Coach Rose out on the football field with Tim Pittsinger. Tim was throwing the shot put and Coach Rose was watching his every move, shouting both instruction and encouragement after each and every toss. Although he had never thrown one himself, Jake knew a shot put weighted a tad more than 16 pounds; the weight of a bowling ball. So what he thought he saw yesterday was true—Tim *was* throwing a bowling ball in his yard, apparently trying to get a feel for how it felt to throw a shot put.

After a 35-minute run, some stretching and a shower Jake couldn't wait to catch up with Tim to find out what he was up to. Jake was a bit surprised to find him still throwing the shot put on the football field, although by this time Coach Rose was nowhere in sight.

'What's up, big guy?' The fact that Jake called Tim 'big guy' was either because he felt comfortable in their relationship or because Jake was still riding high from his good fortune the week before. If you asked Jake he probably wouldn't be able to say for certain, but in all probability it was a little bit of both.

'Let me tell you, Jake. I am so inspired by what you're doing that I thought I'd give this athletic thing a try. I can't run so cross-country and basketball are out, football season is over and I've never had any interest in tennis or golf. Plus I can't swim. But I can throw things really far. So why not give throwing the shot put a try?

Jake couldn't believe the effect he was having on Tim Pittsinger, Blue Harbor's renowned Bad Boy. But he loved every minute of it. *'Keep it up, big guy. I'm proud of you.'*

He would have loved it even more if Tim had mentioned that according to Coach Rose one of his throws that afternoon—63 feet and four inches—was eight inches further than the school record.

An hour later Jake would be home having dinner with his parents. Tim would still be throwing the shot put until the sun went down and it was too dark to see. A shame, actually or he might have been able to tell his final throw was 11 inches better than the school record.

THIRTY – EVERY ROSE HAS ITS THORN

Tuesday morning. What used to be Jake's least favorite day of the week was now near the top of his list, because Tuesday was MEET DAY. And today his friends from Best Foot Forward would be coming over for the first time to watch him run. He wanted to give them something they would be talking about. If he had only known how prophetic that thought had been he might have reconsidered.

When the small bus with 'BFF' painted on either side pulled into the parking lot, Jake interrupted his stretching regimen to rush over to thank them for coming. Dylan was the first one off the bus. Then Mikey, Melissa, four other children he hadn't yet met and finally Miss B. Jake couldn't help but notice all seven of them had a least a hint of both orange and blue in their clothing. *'Hi guys! I'm glad you c-c-c-could make it!' This is going to be GREAT!!!'*

And just like that he was running as fast as he could to join his teammates to hear the last-minute words of Coach Rose.

'Gentlemen. Run hard, run smart and run safe. Most of all run like the wind. One, two, three HERONS!' As they always did, the runners joined Coach Rose for the final cheer, only this time they were louder than usual. Jake couldn't help but think the enthusiasm was because of the seven representatives from Best Foot Forward and the presence of one Timothy Pittsinger who, despite attending Blue Harbor Junior High for almost five years, was attending an athletic event for the very first time. If anyone asked Jake's teammates where the extra enthusiasm came from they would have pointed their fingers at Jake, because this afternoon Jessica Martin was in attendance and Jake had a hard time containing his excitement.

Once the race began Jake stuck to the game plan that had served him so well the last couple of races. At two miles he had a slight lead over Eric Shay and one of the runners from Athens Junior High who seemed to be making one final push with just over 800 meters left in the race. By the time they all got to the final turn they were running side-by-side. The course took a sharp right at that point and Jake was on the right so he could run the tangents, something JD reminded him to do time and time again. Eric was to Jake's left and sandwiched between Jake and the runner from Athens. However as the three made the turn the runner from Athens veered too sharply to his right, bumping Eric who in turn bumped into Jake, forcing him to run off the path, trip over the root of a rather large tree and crash to the ground face first.

Eric and the runner from Athens continued on their way as Jake was rolling over on his back and grabbing his left ankle. Not only had Jake's race come to a sudden halt, the rest of his season was in jeopardy. Coach Rose, who saw everything from his spot near the finish line ran the stretch of 150 meters to tend to his fallen warrior…almost as fast as Eric Shay ran that same distance (albeit in a different direction) and finishing two steps ahead of the Athens runner.

'Tell me what hurts, Jake.' Coach Rose knew what had happened so he didn't need to ask; instead he got right to the point.

'C-c-c-coach, it's my ankle. I think it might be broken.'

Coach Rose had been around long enough and seen enough injuries to know this was nothing more than a sprained ankle. He had also been around long enough to know that for a runner like Jake a sprained ankle was a major catastrophe.

'I think you just sprained your ankle when you went down, Jake. Nothing that a little RICE won't cure.' Coach Rose was always saying how he wished he had a nickel for every time he said that during his 36-year coaching career.

'But c-c-c-coach, I'm not really too k-k-k-keen on eating rice.' Jake was shaking as he spoke, more so because he had never been seriously injured before rather than his anxiety over having to eat rice to get well.

'No, Jake. R-I-C-E. Rest, ice, compression and elevate. That's what you'll need to do for the next week or so. Rest your ankle and don't put a lot of weight and stress on it. Ice your ankle to keep the swelling down. Compress your ankle

by taping it and keeping it as immobile as possible. Elevate your foot by sitting on your couch and propping it above your waist. R-I-C-E. RICE.'

'So if I do all of that I'll be back running by next week?' Coach Rose noticed the corners of Jake's mouth showed the slightest hint of optimism, a sure indication that this young man wanted to *run!*

'You bet, son. Just take it easy, be patient and before you know it you'll be back out here with your teammates in time to regain your stride by the time we compete in the county meet. You've just got to have faith.'

Jake focused on that last word. *'Faith.'* He knew it sounded familiar but he couldn't figure out why.

Jessica ran up just in time to see a huge smile on Jake's face, making her wonder if he was even hurt in the first place. If he was, he sure wasn't showing any signs of it now.

If Jessica only knew: The smile wasn't because Jake wasn't hurt; the smile was because after 36 years of doing it, Coach Rose knew what he was doing.

THIRTY-ONE – FAITH

J ake was determined to make the most of his free time. He had a hard time thinking of it as 'free time' because he felt like he was being held hostage inside his house. He was not able to get outside and do what came naturally to him: Run. He invited Jessica to go with him to Best Foot Forward to meet Miss B and some of the gang he was now spending more and more time with. Jessica, always open to a reason to spend time with Jake was quick to say yes.

The instant they walked through the front door they were surrounded, something Jake had grown accustomed to already. For Jessica, however, this was a brand new experience…and she loved every second of it. Outside of the first time she kissed the boy of her dreams on Valentine's Day, this was the most amazing moment of her life. The children of Best Foot Forward had that effect on her. They had that effect on *everyone*.

Jake grabbed Jessica's hand and told those who had gathered that he wanted to introduce his friend to Miss B, about the same time Sandy Bowers came through the front door and removed the bicycle helmet from her head. *'Hi Jake! And who do we have with us this fine day?'*

Jessica held out her hand. *'I'm Jessica Martin, Jake's girlfriend.'* Jake made a mental note of Jessica saying that publicly for the first time; at least as far as he knew it was the first time. *'I've heard so much about you.'*

'All good, I hope! Do you both have some time to talk? I've got some hot chocolate and if the kids left me any while I was riding, a couple of pastries.' Miss B's sincerity didn't leave much room to say no.

Jake and Jessica followed Sandy Bowers into her office and sat next to one another on the couch while Miss B went to the corner to prepare some

87

hot chocolate. Once three cups were poured she grabbed a tray of pastries and placed everything on the coffee table. *'Help yourselves!'*

It took all of three minutes for Jessica to see why her boyfriend thought the world of Miss B. *'That woman could charm a turtle out of its shell,'* she thought to herself.

Meanwhile Jake's eyes were darting around the office from one sign to another. He knew the background of most with one exception. He looked at Miss B and when he had her attention pointed to the sign in question and asked about it.

'What's the meaning of that one?' he asked.

'Faith in every child? That one was passed along by JD. I always want to call him Mr. Douglas but he insists on JD. Anyway, Faith was the name of his mother. Has he ever told you much about his family?' It was evident there was a story to be told; a story Jake was unfamiliar with.

'He hasn't said much about himself. He's always talking about others and how much he enjoys their company. He's always been able to find something positive in everyone, it seems.' As the words were leaving Jake's mouth, it surprised him how little he really knew about his friend and mentor.

'If you've got some time...'

Jake and Jessica practically answered in unison. *'We do!'*

'Let me refresh your cups and I'll tell you a little something about our mutual friend.'

After a quick refill Miss B told Jake and Jessica the story of Jefferson Saine Douglas.

'As I said Faith was JD's mother. JD never really knew his father because he passed away while JD was still in diapers. Cancer, I believe. His mother held down two full time jobs and worked part time at another on most weekends to make ends meet. JD spent a lot of time with his aunts and uncles growing up because his mother was working most of her waking hours. The hours she had with JD were spent going over his homework with him, teaching him manners and making certain he understood the importance of always doing the absolute best in everything he did. No matter what, his mother expected him to always put his best foot forward.'

Miss B had Jake and Jessica's full attention. *'Tell us more!'* Miss B smiled because it sounded as if Jessica was practically *begging* for the story to continue.

'From an early age JD liked to run. Every day and every night—remember she was working two or more jobs—when he saw his mother come home from his perch on the front porch of his relatives' houses he would make a bee-line to give her a hug before she cleaned up and went back to her other job. As JD got older he became more and more of a runner—remember this was back in a time when there weren't a whole lot of people running—and eventually he became a part of Blue Harbor history when he developed into one of the fastest high school runners in the state. Of course his mother was his biggest cheerleader. JD was so talented he earned a full athletic scholarship at a major university and of course made his mother very proud. Then tragedy struck. On the night before JD was going to compete in the State Cross-Country Meet—he had already won the County and Regional championships at the 5K distance—his mother suffered a brain aneurysm and passed away that very same evening. JD was so distraught he didn't compete in the State meet; in fact he never ran another step after that day; he simply had too much difficulty separating running from his mother's death.

'You are NOT going to stop there!' Jessica was surprised at herself for being so…so demanding. But then again she felt like Miss B and she were old friends, so…

'Of course not. When JD's mother died she wasn't even 50 years old. JD always said she worked herself to death and from what I hear that might not be too far from the truth. He never forgot what his mother taught him. JD always thought his grandparents gave their daughter the name Faith for a reason: She had faith in every man, woman and child to be the best they could possibly be. She always saw the good in people. JD gets that ideology from his mother. So at the time of her death JD was maybe 17 or 18 years old, living alone in his mother's house and holding down a job after school when suddenly he had--a 'revelation,' as he calls it—the vision to create Best Foot Forward so children less fortunate would have a fighting chance in this world…to show them that someone cared about them…to let them know they mattered. Just as his mother had always done for him.'

Miss B took a dramatic pause, causing Jake and Jessica in unison to cry out *'MORE!'* After a brief smile, she did just that.

'You've heard the expression to describe a generous person as someone who would give you the shirt off their back? Well, JD was so generous he gave up the roof over his head. At this very moment you are sitting in the bedroom JD

had as a child. Yes, this is Faith Douglas' house, the house JD grew up in. The house we now call 'Best Foot Forward.'

On the way home Jake and Jessica walked through the park, hoping to bump into JD. They found him entertaining a gathering of squirrels with a small bag of peanuts. Jake walked up to JD, wrapped his arms tightly around his waist and hung on for dear life.

Jake never said a word. He didn't have to; JD had a pretty good idea what was going on since he noticed the two of them had come from the direction of Best Foot Forward.

That, and the tear falling from the corner of Jake's left eye told him everything he needed to know.

THIRTY-TWO — SIDELINE VIEW

I t was absolutely killing Jake to sit idly by while his teammates were competing their hearts out.

Eric Shay ran the best race of his life, easily outdistancing the top runners from each of the schools in today's meet. The other Blue Harbor runners were giving them a run for their money as well. Blue Harbor ended the 5,000-meter run with three of the top five finishes when all was said and done.

About the same time the runners headed into the woods for their second tour of the Heron's Lap, Tim Pittsinger was launching the shot put into orbit: A county record throw of almost 66 feet from a young man who had been throwing the shot put for less than a month. While the majority of the fans in attendance were eagerly awaiting the runners at the finish line, Jake sat in silence as he watched his friend Tim dominate the shot put competition. That is until Tim's county record throw of almost 66 feet, because at that particular moment Jake went wild! *Way to go, big man! I knew you had it in you!*

Tim walked over to Jake and placed his hand on his shoulder. *'Thanks, little buddy. I owe a lot of this to you. Seeing you do so well running against the so-called big boys from the other schools really struck a nerve with me. If you can do so well with that scrawny little body of yours I figured my body had to be good for something other than bouncing kids back and forth in the Pitts.'*

Jake began taking copious mental notes he had every intention of writing down when he got back home later:

- Tim called me 'little buddy.' I guess that makes him my 'big buddy.'
- Tim is actually doing an 'extracurricular activity' that doesn't require someone needing first aid afterwards. That's a comforting thought.
- Could this actually be the 'new and improved' version of the biggest bully in the history of Blue Harbor Junior High?

Jake had no idea what to expect next from the oldest, biggest and up until *now baddest* kid enrolled in Blue Harbor Junior High School.

But what he did realize was this: You have to have faith in people to be the best they can possibly be.

Just like JD's mother always said.

When Jake got home that night he summarized all of his thoughts from the day's events into a single sentence that he wrote on the grease board above the desk in his room:

You'll never know what might have been if you don't give it your best.

Jake went to sleep hoping, no *praying* it wouldn't be long before he was able to run again.

Although he didn't sleep as well as he would have liked, had he known that moment would be only a few days away he more than likely would have slept a little bit better than he actually did.

THIRTY-THREE – C-C-C-CONVICTION

J ake woke up Saturday morning feeling better than he had since his injury. There was no meet today as it was an 'off week' leading up to the county meet in two weekends. Although it had been a couple of weeks since he had met JD at their regular meeting spot—the bench at the front of Central Park—they picked up right where they left off the last time they were together. Only this time words were spoken.

'I'm sorry about your mother. Your father too, but mostly your mother.' The minute Jake said it he knew he stuck his foot in his mouth, implying one parent was more important than the other.

'My father was a good man. It was that gosh darn cancer that did him in. I miss them terribly and there's not a day that goes by that I don't wonder what they would think of Best Foot Forward. I just hope I made them both proud... especially my mother.'

Jake felt a certain degree of forgiveness hearing JD single out his mother over his father as he himself had done earlier. Then again Jake wondered if JD was intentionally doing it to make him feel a little less guilty for doing so.

'I c-c-c-can't help but think they're VERY proud of you, JD. You gave up your home to enrich the lives of others. You've poured your heart and soul into helping others. I'd bet not a day goes by that they aren't smiling down from heaven.'

'I hope you're right, son.' Jake detected a slight bit of doubt in JD's eyes. *'I just hope and pray you're right.'*

'Count on it.' Jake was so intent on getting his message across to JD... making his friend find peace and comfort in the direction his life had taken

that he failed to notice he didn't stutter on a word pronounced with a hard 'C' at the beginning of it.

But JD did. *'Did you just hear yourself, Jake? You said the word 'count' and didn't stutter! Not once.'* JD could tell by the surprise in Jake's eyes that he hadn't noticed.

'It looks to me all you needed was a tiny dose of conviction to get over that stuttering hurdle in your path. I've never heard you say anything as forceful as when you told me to 'count on it' a second ago. I appreciate the thought and for that I thank you. But right now I'm more excited for you than anything else. Keep talking—let's see if you've got any other tricks up your sleeve.'

For the next 20 minutes Jake talked while JD sipped his morning coffee. A sly smile crossed JD's face every time Jake didn't stumble over a word beginning with a hard 'c.' Sure, there were occasional lapses (*'c-c-cross-country'*) but it was a noticeable improvement. Listening to Jake speak with conviction and not stumble over his words nearly as much as before warmed JD's heart as much as the coffee warmed his body.

JD liked this new version of Jake; a young boy full of confidence and conviction and ready to take on the world. JD looked to the sky, a reflex of his when he sought his late mother's approval…a reflex he had since her death over a half century ago.

THIRTY-FOUR – HOPE

Jake stopped by Best Foot Forward on the way home to talk to Miss B about his conversation with JD…his recovery from injury…the breakthrough with his stuttering. It seemed like his world was spinning and he needed someone to talk to about it. Jake's momentum slowed down for a moment when Melissa met him at the door and told him 'Miss B and the boys' were out for a ride on their bicycles, but his momentum picked right back up when he started unloading on Happy Burger's Number One Employee.

'Melissa, I feel like I'll be back running at full strength really soon. Not only that; my stuttering isn't nearly as bad as before. JD thinks it's only a matter of time until I don't stutter at all. Did you know JD was quite a runner when he was my age? I feel bad that he never ran again after he lost his mother. Did you know he lost his mother when he was only a few years older than I am now? I can't imagine how he must have felt, having already lost his father and all.'

As Jake paused to catch his breath, Melissa took the opportunity to comment. *'I've known JD for all of my life. He is probably the wisest man I know. If JD thinks your stutter will be gone, it will be. He said the same thing about mine, even when he patiently listened to me because it took me so long to say certain things—you don't know how many words you use beginning with the letter 'f' until you have a difficult time saying them—but over time and with JD's encouragement I was able to get through it. Now if I could only add another four inches to my short leg I could get out there and run with you!'*

Jake couldn't decide if a chuckle or even a smile was appropriate, so he stuck with nodding his head. Melissa could tell Jake didn't know what to make of her comment about running with him, so she tried to lighten things up by saying *'Come on Jake—I'm joking around with you! It's OK to laugh once in a while!'*

Melissa's comment was just what Jake needed to hear. Jake was always much too serious about things—his parents told him so on more than one occasion—and it took the words of a fellow ninth-grader to make him realize it for himself. Jake thought now was as good a time as any to turn things around.

'I'd love the company…as long as you don't make me look bad!' Jake had a big toothy grin that implied he felt good about his first attempt at humor in a very long time.

Melissa immediately fired back with this: *'Don't worry; I'll promise to take it easy on you!'* The second she finished the sentence both Jake and Melissa had the same thought in their head about wishing that day would come.

For the next 90 minutes the two of them felt as comfortable around one another as two lifelong friends spending time together sharing their innermost thoughts and desires. Jake expressed how much he wanted to make those closest to him proud and that he found his best venue for doing that to be running. Melissa was the same way, as evidenced by the perseverance and effort she demonstrated every time she put on her Happy Burger uniform and reported for work. Although in entirely different ways they showed they were very much alike, and when they both realized that it made them appreciate one another even more.

As Melissa got more and more comfortable being with Jake she hesitated before asking him if he knew the story of the pair of running shoes tied together and draped over the end of the park bench. *'No, I don't believe JD has ever talked about them before.'*

Well aware of the answer before she asked the question, Melissa asked anyway. *'Would you like to hear the story behind the shoes?'* She may as well have asked Jake if he wanted a butterscotch sundae while watching this afternoon's *Creature Feature. 'You know I DO!'* His voice could be heard throughout the building had anyone been there other than the two of them.

'When JD first started running there weren't running shoes available like there are now. There were only basketball and tennis shoes—'sneakers' is what they were called for the most part. One day JD decided he wanted to run in

something other than the basketball shoes belonging to his late father that were a couple of sizes too small for him anyway. So he mowed lawns—and this was when most lawn mowers didn't have motors—to earn enough money to buy a pair of shoes at Happel's, the local discount store in town. The pair he bought—and the pair now hanging on the park bench in Central Park—was nothing more than orange and blue tennis shoes. But JD loved them—probably because they were his school colors—and he wore them proudly up until the day his mother passed. I'm pretty certain he hasn't run a step since that day. He loved those shoes so much he even had a name for them: 'Hope.' Hope, of course reflects his optimistic attitude about achieving a positive outcome. It's also a reference to one of the three saints: Faith, Hope and Charity. His mother's name, of course was Faith. He called his shoes Hope, and when he turned over his home to become what it is today, Best Foot Forward, he felt that he had honored Charity, the third and final saint.'

Jake found the story fascinating. More than that, it gave him an idea.

An idea he thought would both surprise and honor his good friend and mentor Jefferson Saine Douglas. He couldn't wait to get started on it.

THIRTY-FIVE — SPECIAL REQUEST

L ater that night Jake was sitting at his desk in front of his bedroom window. He barely noticed the brilliant luminance of the full moon, seemingly within arm's reach. He had a pen in his hand and a pad of paper on the desk in front of him. He was writing to the president of Mercury Athletics, the company that made the running shoes he'd worn since he was seven years old.

> *Dear Sir or Madam/Creative Consultant (?) at Mercury Athletics,*
>
> *My name is Jake Kerslake. I am a ninth-grader at Blue Harbor Junior High School. I am a runner for our cross-country team that is coached by Bill Rose. He is a really good coach and is teaching me a lot.*
> *I also have a good friend who used to run cross-country for my school a long time ago. His name is Jefferson Douglas, but his friends call him 'JD.' He has been helping me not only with my running, but in my development as a person as well. Unfortunately JD quit running about the time he was my age after he lost his mother. He still has the original pair of shoes he ran in (I am enclosing a photograph of them); they hang on the back of a bench that we sit and talk on almost every Saturday morning.*
> *I was wondering if you made a shoe that looked something like them and if so could I buy a pair of them in size 8? I*

would love to wear them in our county cross-country meet in
a few weeks. It would be a big surprise to JD if I did!
  Thank you for your time.

Jake Kerslake
9ᵗʰ grade, Blue Harbor Junior High School
P.S. JD had a name for his shoes: Hope.

As he signed his name with his left hand he turned off his desk lamp with his right. He jumped into bed and slept sounder than he had since his injury. He was so exhausted from the day's events he totally forgot about the fresh piece of rhubarb pie sitting on the corner of his desk.

THIRTY-SIX – HEALING PROCESS

The week went by faster than Jake could have possibly imagined. Spending quality time with people you love, respect and truly care for tends to make time fly.

And after seven days of meticulously following Coach Rose's advice, Jake's ankle felt better than ever. The county meet was coming up soon, but not soon enough as far as Jake was concerned. He was ready to run…NOW!

But running would have to wait one more day. Coach Rose's original plan was for Jake to return to practice two Mondays before the county meet, so for now he had to focus his burning energy on something other than running. So he took a walk across the street to Central Park to spend some time with his mentor.

As was usually the case, JD was sitting on the park bench feeding (or was he talking to?) the squirrels and sipping on a steaming cup of coffee. *'How's the ankle, my friend?'* Jake could see the hope in JD's eyes of hearing some good news; he couldn't help but smile when he realized he used the word 'hope' in his thoughts about the man who used to run in a pair of shoes he referred to by the same name. The smile turned into a chuckle when he glanced at the pair of orange and blue shoes hanging from one end of the bench.

'What's tickling your innards?' It was obvious JD was genuinely curious about what was making Jake laugh.

'Your shoes, JD. I know you've had them a long time. A very long time, actually and it just dawned on me I've never seen them on your feet.'

'Son, I haven't worn those shoes in over 50 years. I was barely older than you the last time I wore them. Just never had the desire after…well, you know.' A tear was forming in the corners of JD's eyes as his voice trailed off.

'I can't imagine what it was like to lose your parents at such an early age… not to mention your number one fan.' Jake spoke like someone well beyond his years.

JD's eyes lit up. *'You did it again, Jake. You did it again!'*

'Did WHAT, exactly?' It was obvious Jake had no idea what JD was referring to.

'You didn't stutter over the word 'can't.' I'm no expert on the subject, but I do believe when you're passionate about what you're saying—when you put your heart and soul into every word you speak—your stutter becomes a distant memory. It tells me you're gaining confidence in yourself; in your thoughts, actions and beliefs.' If Jake didn't know better he would have thought he was listening to the words of a psychologist.

Jake paused for a minute before speaking: *'I never thought about it that way, JD, but you just might be on to something.'*

'You are turning into one fine young man, and I'm proud to call you my friend.' JD was never more serious in his life when he added: *'If you run with the confidence, the passion and the conviction I know you have inside of you, you're going to run away from everyone in the county meet next Saturday.'*

Jake's eyes lit up with such intensity JD would have sworn he had seen a light bulb turn on above Jake's head. *'Will you come and watch me run next Saturday? It would mean a lot to me. It would mean EVERYTHING to me.'*

'Son, I haven't watched a competitive running event since…well, since. What makes you think I want to come out and watch one NOW?' Had Jake not been looking dejectedly at the ground as JD was speaking he would have noticed the sly smile across JD's face.

'I just…I just thought…' JD could tell by Jake's voice it was time for him to be sincere so he quickly spoke up:

'What I'm trying to say is this: It will be my pleasure to be there. In fact I would be HONORED to watch you run next Saturday! I can't wait to see all of your hard work pay off. Count me in, young Mister Kerslake.'

Jake was quick to correct his elder: *'All of OUR hard work.'*

JD gave Jake a hug and whispered in his ear: *'It's been a privilege. Thank you for allowing me the honor of knowing you.'*

Jake decided right then and there: He was going to prove to Coach Rose he could run with both his heart and his head at the same time.

But more importantly he was going to make JD proud.

THIRTY-SEVEN — CONFIDENCE

I n all of Bill Rose's 36 years of coaching he had never witnessed a week of practice like this week's.

Jake Kerslake was running like the wind and the rest of the Blue Harbor Herons were doing everything in their power to keep up. Coach Rose couldn't find the words to explain how well Jake was running but he did remember a quote he heard many years ago: '*Lions run the fastest when they are hungry.*'

Speaking of hungry, Jake's parents were having a hard time believing their son's suddenly voracious appetite, to say nothing of his willingness to open up at the dinner table every night. The usual 'OK' after David and Alice Kerslake asked their son about his day had been replaced with *Jake* starting the conversation by saying *'you'll never guess what happened at school today!'*

Even Jessica noticed a difference in Jake. It took her a while to put her finger on it, but once she found the right word to describe it she knew exactly what it was: *Confidence.* This wasn't the quiet, timid Jake who was embarrassed so much that his face turned red when she thanked him publicly with a kiss on the cheek after rescuing her cat from a tree many years ago. No, this was a young man who had his hands firmly on the steering wheel driving his future and she, for one was enjoying being along for the ride.

Jake was also having the time of his life in his daily visits to Best Foot Forward after his post-practice shower. Jake was working with Mikey, Dylan and a revolving door of seven or eight other boys and girls who wanted to become runners 'just like Jake.' Jake enjoyed sharing his passion for running and the many hours of wisdom he absorbed from his conversations with JD to his 'little brothers and sisters,' as he often referred to them. Most days he was accompanied by Tim Pittsinger, as Tim's expertise was sought by two of the bigger boys at Best Foot Forward. They mistakenly thought the shot put didn't require much physical effort or ability; Tim put them through several very rigorous workouts until they realized they were wrong. The best outcome of these interactions is that the kids of Best Foot Forward were—like Jake and Tim—growing up and gaining more and more confidence each and every day.

Every day of that week ended the same way: Jake and JD sitting on the park bench, sharing a conversation that didn't usually end until dusk. The topics were many—everything from what it would be like to be a squirrel to the definitive meaning of life—and almost everything in between. There didn't seem to be anything these two men—separated in life by almost three generations and more than half a century—couldn't talk about. Friday evening's conversation ended with JD asking Jake to meet him at the bench the next morning wearing his running gear.

As Jake went home Friday night to watch *Poltergeist* that he recorded while he was at practice, it never dawned on him that JD had never previously asked him to wear his running attire when they met on Saturday morning. If he *had* taken the time to think about it, it may have aroused his curiosity. After all, it certainly had a reason to.

THIRTY-EIGHT — SECOND WIND

Second Wind – A return of strength or energy
making it possible to continue in an activity or start again

Saturday morning couldn't come soon enough. What last-minute advice would JD have as the county meet was now only one week away? What words of wisdom would he have to offer as the biggest day of Jake's running life was going to take place in just seven days?

Jake sprinted all the way to the park bench with the intention of it being a warmup for the morning workout JD was sure to put him through. The first thing he noticed when he got to the park was the pair of orange and blue running shoes draped over one end of the park bench. They were missing.

As was always the case, by the time Jake arrived at the park on Saturday morning, JD was already there. But on this morning Jake noticed something different about JD. He wore his usual gray warmup outfit, had a steaming cup of coffee in his hand and a big smile on his face. He also had a pair of orange and blue running shoes on his feet, the same pair that that had been hanging on the edge of the bench he hadn't worn since he was a student at Blue Harbor Junior High oh-so-many years ago.

'I thought I'd join you for a run this morning. That is, if you don't mind.' JD took one last sip of coffee before tossing the cup into the recycling bin.

'Are you kidding me? Of COURSE I don't mind! Only I thought you never wanted to run again.' It was obvious Jake was both delighted and confused.

'Things change, Jake. You've changed. And now you've changed ME by making me want to run again…to experience the freedom and sheer delight that only running can bring. Deep down inside I always felt I wanted to run again,

but until today I just couldn't. It's as simple as that. But our conversations this week—I recognized the joy you get from running every time you mentioned it and it reminded me so much of myself when I was your age. That's why I picked today to run again…and I can't think of anyone else I'd rather do it with than you.'

More so because he knew if he didn't start running his eyes were likely going to well up with tears, Jake simply motioned to JD and mumbled *'then let's get going!'*

And just like that the two of them took off running stride-for-stride towards an orange sun that appeared to be rising out of the crystal clear waters of Blue Harbor Bay. Ten minutes into their run the sky grumbled before opening up and unleashing a monsoon-like rain. *'Do you want to take shelter?'* Jake asked, not sure if his elder would want to continue being outside in this type of weather.

'Don't shoo away the storm, 'cuz then you can't run in the rain.' Not a word was shared between the two for the rest of their 90-minute run. Jake couldn't help but notice how graceful JD was as he matched him stride-for-stride along the asphalt path around the perimeter of the park; he thought how talented a runner he must have been as a teenager. When they returned to the park bench JD immediately took a seat, smiled and looked up at Jake and said simply: *'Best run ever.'*

Jake couldn't agree more. *'Yep, best run ever.'*

THIRTY-NINE — JONATHAN

Saturday afternoon Jake kept his promise to some of the youngsters at Best Foot Forward and took them out for a two-mile run (with lots of walking) through the park. While none of them were setting the world on fire, Jake noticed two or three of them showed a lot of potential. Jake wondered to himself if they would be running for Coach Rose in another three or four years.

Afterwards Jake stopped in Sandy Bowers' office to invite her to the county meet, now only a week away.

'I think I can make that happen, Jake.' As always Sandy Bowers' smile reflected the sincerity of her answer. *'I'll bet Mikey, Dylan and some of the others would like to come along. Would that be OK?'*

'OK? Sandy—that would be terrific!' Jake could barely contain his excitement. He loved those kids and to think they had an interest in Jake's running was more than he could hope for.

Sandy looked at Jake with the sternest look on her face: *'Did you hear yourself just now, Jake?'*

'Did I say something wrong?' Jake had no idea what she could be referring to.

'You called me Sandy. SANDY!!! Finally! That's just amazing! Sandy couldn't have been more excited had she won the lottery.

'JD has sort of noticed that as well. He said I have more confidence... more conviction, even and it's coming out in the way I speak. I appreciate you noticing! It means a lot to me. JD means a lot to me. YOU mean a lot to me!' Jake was so comfortable with Sandy that he didn't even blush as he told her his true feelings about her.

'If I know JD—and I have for many, many years—I imagine he had something to do with it. He is quite a man. I'm sure you can see why he means so much to me.' Sandy had the same look on her face as she always did when she spoke about JD; one of love, respect and admiration.

Sandy continued. *'Did JD ever tell you about his brother Jonathan? He was the original inspiration for Best Foot Forward.'*

'I didn't even know JD had a brother.' NOW Jake was just the slightest bit embarrassed. *'Where is he now?'*

'Sadly Jonathan is no longer with us. He was born with cerebral palsy, a movement disorder that usually appears in early childhood. Back when Jonathan and JD were young the consequences were much more severe than they are today. Of course now there is a lot more care and assistance available. JD loved his brother; if JD wasn't running he was either playing with Jonathan, reading to him or simply taking care of him. Jonathan was the younger brother and when he passed away, JD was devastated; shortly afterwards he dedicated his life to helping children in need. That's why he put everything he had into establishing Best Foot Forward...why he has a special place in his heart for children with challenges...why he has sacrificed his life for them. If you ask him if he has any regrets he'll tell you he only has one: That he had to say goodbye to everyone in his family—his father, his mother and his little brother. JD never married and is now the only remaining member of the Davis family.'

Whenever Sandy spoke about JD's life, she always had Jake's full attention. This time was no different than any other time unless you take into account the tears rolling down Jake's bright red cheeks, because that was a first. When Sandy Bowers did the same, it was another first.

Little did they know more tears were on the way for both of them. Many more.

FORTY – GRACE

f there was one thing you could count on Alice Kerslake for, it was to say
grace before every meal. Dinnertime was her favorite as it allowed a time
to give thanks for the day's events and pray for good things to happen in
the future. It was always a given that grace would be offered by the woman
in the house at the Kerslake residence.

That's why it surprised both husband and wife when their only son
offered to say thanks on a rainy Saturday night in the second week of
spring. The calendar said it was spring but the weather outside suggested
otherwise: Cold, rainy and a westerly wind that made the temperature feel
20 degrees colder than it actually was.

'Mom, if you don't mind I'd like to say grace tonight.' The words
couldn't sound any better to Alice Kerslake had they been sung by angels
accompanied by a four-piece ensemble of stringed instruments.

Alice Kerslake replied without a hint of hesitation: *'By all means,
please do.'*

As all three members of the Kerslake family bowed their heads, Jake began:

> *'Dear Lord, we thank you. Thank you for this meal we are
> about to enjoy, thank you for the courage and strength to make
> it through another day and thank you for all you do. Please
> look after each and every one of us, and if you can find it in
> your heart keep a close eye on Miss B and the children of Best
> Foot Forward. I would really appreciate it. They mean and
> give a lot to me and I wish I could do more for them in return.
> Look after Coach Rose and our team as we prepare this last*

111

week before the biggest cross-country meet of the season. And please watch over my good friend JD, the kindest and most generous man I have ever met. Thank you for giving him the strength to run with me this morning. He showed me what it means to put your best foot forward and for that I will be always be grateful. Now bless this meal we are able to receive, because I AM STARV-ING!'

It was a good thing Jake ended on a slightly humorous note; otherwise the men at the table may have noticed Alice Kerslake's eye makeup streaming down the sides of her face.

FORTY-ONE – LIGHTNING STRIKES

Although they hadn't made any plans to meet, Jake decided to stop by and see if JD might be feeding the squirrels at the park bench as he went out for his Sunday morning run. The sky was clear for the first time in a couple of days although the dampness in the air made it feel much colder than it actually was. Jake made his way into the park when he noticed some flashing red lights in the vicinity of the park bench.

As he got closer and closer to the bench he noticed he was getting closer and closer to the flashing red lights as well. Jake had a strange feeling in his stomach when he discovered an ambulance and two police cars surrounding the park bench with the orange and blue pair of shoes hanging on one end. This strange feeling wasn't the jitters; it was something far, far worse.

'Good morning, son. Is there anything we can do for you?' The policeman sensed something was wrong with Jake and wanted to help if he could.

'I was just looking for my friend JD. He's usually here most mornings feeding the squirrels.'

'You must mean Mister Douglas. He was a fine man; I've known him for years. I'm sorry to tell you this but Mister Douglas passed away during the night. We found him on his bench this morning.' The compassion the policeman had for both JD and his young friend was evident in his voice.

'JD…JD is gone? We just ran together yesterday. He said it was his best run ever. He…he's GONE?' Jake couldn't believe his ears. JD was a model of fitness, not to mention one of the finest men he had ever met. He just COULDN'T be gone. *'Are you sure?'* Tears began streaming down Jake's face at the realization of losing his best friend was starting to sink in.

'I'm sorry to say that it's true. Mister Douglas was just placed inside of that ambulance right over there.' The policeman nodded in the direction of the ambulance as he spoke. *'We got a phone call from a woman walking her dog this morning. Apparently he passed away in his sleep during the night.'*

'In his sleep?' Jake was confused. *'Then how did he get to the park?'*

'Oh, I guess you didn't know. Mister Douglas lived here in the park. It's what he called home. The park bench was his bed. Has been ever since I was in high school. He always said all he needed was a couple of dollars to eat and a place to rest his head at night. Heard he donated almost everything he had to establish Best Foot Forward. Darnedest thing I've ever heard of, if you ask me. Darn nice fellow. I'm proud just to have known him.'

Jake was stunned. He had no idea that JD didn't have somewhere to go home to each night…that he had been sleeping outside on these cold, bitter nights…that he had nowhere to hang his hat…that he chose to be homeless so he could help others. As close as the two of them had grown, how had he *not noticed?* Jake doubted himself, wondering if he even had the right to call himself JD's friend. The pain in his stomach grew more intense.

The policeman spoke up. *'Don't be sad, young man. JD loved living under the stars. He loved the fresh air, the smell of the trees, the sound of children playing, the change of the seasons. The man simply loved life. I'm sure you noticed those things.'*

Jake analyzed every word as the policeman spoke. Yes, he had noticed those things about his friend; he just never put them all together to realize that JD lived his life in the true spirit of putting his best foot forward by helping others the best way he knew how.

Jake's stomach was calming down slightly as he began to understand the life of the man known as Jefferson Saine Douglas. It would be a long time, however before he understood why his life had to come to an end.

FORTY-TWO – RAINY SEASON

After learning of JD's death, Jake didn't know what to do next. Instinct took over and he did the thing he did best: He ran.

In fact he ran the exact same route he had run with JD 24 hours earlier. Jake was subconsciously afraid that if he stopped running he would break down and cry. So he ran the entire route three times and was heading out for a fourth when he heard someone calling his name.

It was Jessica, who had recently started running primarily because of the influence of the boy next door. She knew the moment she saw Jake's face that something was wrong.

'JD...he's gone.' Jake had been right; the minute he stopped he broke down and cried.

'What do you mean he's gone?' Jessica thought the worst but hoped for the best—maybe JD had gone on vacation or worst case moved to another town.

'He died in his sleep. He was sleeping on the park bench over there. Jessica, he was just sleeping on the bench...' His voice trailed off and he wept again.

Jessica wrapped her arms around Jake. She noticed he was trembling and correctly assumed it was not because of the cold weather. *'I'm so sorry, Jake. I know what he meant to you. He was a good friend. YOU were a good friend. I know you'll miss him.'*

Jake took comfort in the warmth of her body and the sincerity in her voice: Truer words were never spoken.

'I do miss him, Jessica. I miss him...BAD!' And with that Jake wept again as rain started falling from the sky. The wet skies made Jessica imagine Jake wasn't the only one weeping over JD's passing.

In all probability she was probably right.

FORTY-THREE – THE DULDRUMS

Doldrum — a state of listlessness or despondency

Dinner on Sunday evening at the Kerslake residence was the most solemn it had ever been. Jake didn't have an appetite and his parents couldn't seem to find the words to comfort their teenage son. In fact Jake asked to be excused before dessert was served; Alice Kerslake couldn't remember the last time *that* happened.

At school Monday morning Jake's classmates offered their sympathy one-by-one. Eric Shay and Tim Pittsinger were the first ones to do so; in fact they met him as he got off the bus in front of the school. Jake's other teammates expressed their remorse throughout the day—they all knew of the relationship between Jake and his friend and mentor—but all of the support from his peers did little to lighten his spirit. When all was said and done JD was still gone; there was nothing that could change that simple fact.

At the beginning of practice Coach Rose took Jake aside and asked him how he was doing. Words weren't needed for the veteran coach to know Jake wasn't doing well; that was evident by how sluggish Jake performed in practice. Coach Rose made a mental note: *'There is a very definite possibility I will have to pull Jake out of Saturday's county championship if he doesn't show any drive by the end of the week. Right now his heart just ain't in it.'* Tuesday and Wednesday's practice sessions did little to change his mind.

Little did Coach Rose know that a small band of special needs children and one very extraordinary woman were about to do something to change his mind very, very soon. It just so happened that Jake had been invited by his friends at Best Foot Forward to join them for dinner.

Well, dinner and a little something extra.

FORTY-FOUR — GAME CHANGER

'*Happy Hump Day, Jake!*' Jake couldn't believe his eyes when he walked through the front door of Best Foot Forward and was greeted with a rousing welcome from more kids than he could ever remember seeing at one time. Jake, still distraught over the passing of his good friend didn't even connect the dots…'Hump Day' meant it was Wednesday and the county meet was now less than three days away.

Sandy Bowers entered the room and invited everyone to take a seat around the long dining room table. Once all 24 seats were occupied and Miss B made sure no one was left out, she tapped a spoon on the side of her glass of water to gain everyone's attention.

'*I'd like to welcome our special guest this evening, our good friend Jake Kerslake. As you all know Jake and JD were the best of friends. Sadly JD won't get to see Jake run in person this Saturday at the county meet, but I know in my heart he'll be watching from above. As for everyone in this room, we'll be loading up the BFF bus Saturday morning at 8 a.m. so we can get to the county meet by 9 a.m. and watch Jake run. How does that sound to everyone?*'

With the exception of Jake, everyone in the room cheered. Jake simply made a mental note that he would be running soon, although it did nothing to light any type of fire inside of him.

'*Jake, you'll be glad to know we spoke to your mom. She told us you really like meat loaf, mashed potatoes and lima beans. I'll bet you can't guess what we're having this evening!*' Sandy Bowers' eyes were twinkling, as they were prone to do whenever she was excited about something.

Melissa and Cheryl, an eleven-year with autism had the honor of serving dinner. Throughout the course of the meal the children tried to engage Jake in conversation in hopes of raising his spirits and getting him excited about his big race on Saturday. Nothing seemed to matter up until the time the rhubarb pie was brought out for dessert. Because that's when Dylan spoke up loud enough for everyone to hear:

'Jake, you probably don't know this but JD has done something for every single one of us in this room to make our lives better. Saturday you're going to realize what he's done for you—I guarantee you that!' Young Dylan spoke with the wisdom and confidence of someone five times his age.

For the first time since the loss of JD, Jake actually listened. In fact from that point on he continued listening throughout the evening as one child after another spoke to him about their relationship with JD and what he had personally done to enrich their lives. Jake's admiration for JD grew in leaps and bounds to the point that he actually began looking forward to running in the county meet to honor his late friend. Jake could feel the fire burning in his stomach by the time Miss B called him into her office for one last surprise.

'Jake, before JD passed away he asked me to hold onto several envelopes and distribute them when he was gone. One letter was addressed to the children of Best Foot Forward and was read to them last night. He thanked them for making him feel useful and fulfilling his dream of helping others and making a difference. One letter was addressed to me. I'm humbled by how much he thought of me; tears were running down my face by the time I got to the end of it. He said what was left of his life savings would be turned over to me and should be used for keeping this house on the path of helping others. I intend to honor his wishes 100%! A third letter he left for you. You can take it home or read it here in private. Your choice!'

'If you don't mind I'd like you to read it now. I need to hear his words one more time, and I can't think of anyone I'd rather hear them from than you.' The calmness in Jake's voice was not indicative of the anticipation in his heart.

'It would be my pleasure.' Sandy Bowers had never been more sincere in her life. After a deep breath she carefully opened the envelope and began reading the letter Jefferson Douglas had carefully written by hand.

My dear, dear friend Jake,

My how you have grown since I first met you running from a boy whom you would later befriend. That same day your talent as a runner was discovered and it changed your life for what I believe will be forever. You've developed your talent for running by listening to the people whom have always had your best interests at heart. You are wise beyond your years in that respect, and it has served you well. Of all the runners I have known in my life I've never seen anyone with more raw talent than you, Jake. Beyond that of all the people I have known in my life you rank right up there with the inspirational Sandy Bowers in terms of how much you care for your fellow man. The way ALL of the children of Best Foot Forward made an instant connection with you is testimony enough for me to say that.

Do good things with your life, Jake Kerslake. Don't ever take 'no' for an answer; there are always ways to make things happen, to get things done…that's how you change the world. Find them and show the world what you're capable of. You're definitely one of a kind. I am a better man for knowing you; I hope you can one day say the same about me. If that is the case I can die a happy man. I've had a good life—not what others might call a good life but one that I'm more than satisfied with. I leave this planet with good friends and good memories and for that I am grateful.

Most of all remember to always put your best foot forward in everything you do. Make a difference with your life. Make a difference in someone's life. Most of all: Make a difference!

I will always be with you, Jake Kerslake. Don't ever forget that.

I wish you the very best for all the days of your life. I will forever remain your friend.

Jefferson

Sandy Bowers folded up the letter, stuck it back inside the envelope and handed it to Jake. Jake put the envelope in his back right pocket, hugged Miss B good night and headed for the front door.

Once outside he ran all the way home, faster than he had run since his injury.

After all he had a wish to fulfill: Someone wanted him to put his best foot forward. There was not a better time to start than tonight.

FORTY-FIVE – A GLIMMER OF HOPE

J ake had his best practice of the season Thursday afternoon and it couldn't have come at a better time: Two days before the county meet. Coach Rose was impressed; the other boys on the team were downright intimidated. None of them had ever seen anyone run with such fire, emotion and reckless abandon than Jake Kerslake on an overcast, unseasonably cool spring afternoon in Blue Harbor.

As the boys piled into the locker room Coach Rose met them with the slightest hint of a smile that he expressed verbally with a simple *good job, men.'* On the inside, however his stomach was doing somersaults. He was more than pleased with the performance of the team; he was downright *ecstatic.* It was all he could do to suppress his true emotions in front of the team, but being the veteran coach he was he somehow managed.

After the boys showered and dressed and headed out of the locker room to start on their homework, study for an exam or stop by Happy Burger— to each his own, Coach Rose always said—Jake was stopped in his tracks when the veteran coach called his name and asked him to stop by his office.

Jake entered the tiny office of his coach, closed the door and spotted a well-dressed man sitting on one of the three aluminum chairs surrounding the mismatched desk pushed towards the back of the room. *'Jake, this is Bill Day. He's responsible for marketing for Mercury Athletics. He has something he'd like to talk to you about.'*

Jake remembered the letter he had written as Bill Day began to speak.

'Jake, I was very impressed with you out there today.' Jake hadn't noticed the well-dressed gentleman sitting in the bleachers as they were running, either because of how overcast it had been or because the team was too

focused on their last hard work out before the county meet, although in all probability it was the latter. *'Speaking for all of us at Mercury Athletics, we were impressed with your letter. It would be our honor for you to wear this pair of shoes Saturday in your county meet.'*

As he spoke Bill Day held up a brand new pair of orange and blue running shoes—in a size eight, of course and handed them to Jake. *'We're calling them simply 'Hope.' Go ahead; try them on!'*

Jake had his tennis shoes pulled off before Bill Day finished his sentence. He excitedly put them on his feet, tied the laces and left the office to run up and down the hall. After five or six jogs to the end of the hall he came back inside the office and sat down in his chair. *'Wearing them is like running on air. I LOVE them!'*

'Then that's a good thing because they're yours. We would be honored if you would run in them Saturday morning. I think your friend JD would be honored as well.'

'You knew JD?' Jake's mind flashed back to the summer after second grade when his parents took him to Disney World and the song *It's a Small World* stuck in his head for weeks afterwards.

'Actually I did, Jake. Sort of, anyway. My father ran against him many, many years ago. He said he was the best he'd ever seen. Smooth, fluid, graceful and quick as a cat. I hear JD said similar things about you. Would you believe my dad still talks about him every now and then. In a 'what if' kind of way, as in what if he stuck with running after the tragedies he experienced in his youth. He probably would have run for our country in the Olympics. Or maybe won the Boston Marathon. Guess we'll never know. Too bad, actually.'

'Yeah, it sure is' Jake said aloud, although his mind was racing with a litany of thoughts swirling around inside his brain. However the thought his mind was able to focus on was this: *'Saturday I'm going to make JD proud, I just KNOW it!'*

Jake left Coach Rose's office feeling more confident than he ever had in his life.

It made it hard to believe that less than 24 hours earlier the county meet was barely a blip on Jake's radar.

What a difference a day makes. That thought was in the back of Jake's mind as he turned in for the night. For Coach Rose it was the only thought.

But the one thought they both shared was this: Saturday was going to be something special.

Before turning in for the night Jake silently read his note from JD. A single tear fell as he got to the last sentence: *I will forever remain your friend.*

Jake would drift off to sleep that night with a hole in his heart…as wide as the Mississippi River.

FORTY-SIX — AN OLD FRIEND

The cross-country boys from Blue Harbor had their Friday afternoon free for the first time since the Christmas holidays. This was a tradition of Coach Rose's: Let the boys rest on the night before the county meet. It was a good plan…as long as the boys did what Coach wanted them to do: Rest.

Of course there were some who wanted to take advantage of their free afternoon skateboarding, going to the mall or playing in a pickup basketball game at the playground in Central Park. If it weren't for that nasty broken ankle suffered by Will Harris when he tried doing a 360 on his skateboard seven years ago Coach Rose would have never been the wiser about the boys daring to do anything other than rest. So thanks to Will Harris he reminded the team after Thursday's practice that they had better take his advice seriously. Or else.

Fortunately no one in the past seven years wanted to find out what Coach Rose meant by 'or else,' so they did what he asked. They rested.

As Jake was resting on his front porch Friday evening a car pulled into his driveway. A distinguished looking elderly gentleman got out of the car, looked at Jake and asked if this was the Kerslake household.

'It sure is. What can I do for you?' Jake assumed the gentleman was looking for his father; perhaps his mother. The gentleman's reply took him totally by surprise.

'I'm here to see you, Jake. My name is Terry Bowers. You know my granddaughter Sandy. She speaks very highly of you.'

Jake perked up instantly. *'Sandy is GREAT! I love spending time with the kids over at Best Foot Forward. I owe Sandy a lot for opening her doors to me.'*

129

'Thank you. She speaks highly of you as well. Apparently you and JD make a great team.'

Jake's eyes lit up the moment Mister Bowers spoke JD's name. *'You used to run with JD!'*

Realizing Jake was interested in hearing about his late friend's exploits when he was a boy Terry Bowers held Jake's attention for the next 90 minutes as he recounted one story after another with tales about running with JD. There was the time they ran to Cedar River…the time they chased after (and caught) a neighbor's dog that escaped from the back yard…the time they ran from midnight to sunrise just to see if they could. Jake could sense the elderly gentleman's passion for running just by the expression on his face as he spoke.

Terry Bowers could sense that same passion for running simply by the look in Jake's eyes as he spoke. He could also sense—correctly so—the love and admiration Jake had for his late friend. *'I'm going to miss ole Jefferson. I can't tell you how much I'm going to miss our dinner and catch-up time every Tuesday night.'*

Jake had no idea JD and Mister Bowers had stayed in touch all this time, or that the reason JD couldn't attend his Tuesday meets was because two old friends were having dinner together. Then again, it wasn't like JD talked about himself very often; he was much more interested in talking about his close personal friends. That's just the kind of person he was.

'I thought you might like to have this, Jake. It's something JD gave me a long time ago.' Terry Bowers handed something to Jake that was hidden in the palm of his hand.

Jake took it in his hand and examined the small silver medallion with 'BFF' inscribed on the front and 'Always, Jefferson' on the back. *'I can't take this, Mister Bowers.'*

'Sure you can, Jake. He was your friend too.'

Hearing that, Jake didn't waste any time placing the chain around his neck and centering the medallion on his chest. He glanced at the BFF inscription once more, looked up at Terry Bowers and softly said: *'Yes, he was my friend too.'*

The two shook hands as Mister Bowers closed the conversation. *'Indeed he was. By the way, watch your step tomorrow in the county meet. That course in Radford can be tricky if you're not careful. Good luck, Jake.'*

FORTY-SEVEN – PLAYING IN THE RAIN

Maybe it was out of habit. Then again maybe it was a silent tribute to his late friend. Whatever the reason, at 5:30 a.m. on the Saturday of the county meet Jake made himself a cup of hot chocolate and brewed a cup of coffee for...*who*, exactly? His parents weren't awake, JD was gone and he didn't drink coffee. As he poured the coffee into the sink it reminded him how much he wanted JD to see him run today. Sure, Sandy Bowers and the kids from Best Foot Forward would be there. So would Jessica and his parents. Tim Pittsinger was even going to be there.

But not the person Jake wanted to be there most of all. Today Jefferson Douglas would be there in spirit only.

By the time Jake walked out his front door at 7:00 to head to Blue Harbor Junior High to board the bus that would take the team to the county meet, the skies opened up and produced monsoon-like wind and rain that would certainly make running on the 3.1-mile circuit an adventure; a wet, muddy adventure. Once he got to the school parking lot and boarded the bus, Jake found his teammates to be in direct contrast to the dark and dreary day. In fact they were just the opposite: Light-spirited and full of energy, as if they intended on taking *control* of this day despite weather that showed no signs of cooperating with the event about to unfold.

This year's county meet was held on the cross-country course—three laps on a worn trail of slightly over one mile around the campus of Radford Junior High that was certain to be ankle-deep in water by the start of the race.

Coach Rose reminded the team as the bus pulled into the parking lot what he expected from each and every one of them this morning:

'First, remember all the hard work you've put in this year to get to this point. You've earned the right to be here. You DESERVE to be here. Second, run your own race. All of you have your own distinctive style and game plan; it is now up to you. Third, cover the path in front of you to the best of your ability. And finally, I'm darn proud of each and every one of you. Win, lose or draw this season has been a blast. Let's end it on a high note. One we'll remember for a very long time. Alright, everyone in. Goooooooooooooooooooooooo HERONS!'

After a few strides in a pouring rain, Jake made his way to the starting line between two rather large oak trees, mere saplings when JD and Terry Bowers ran the same route many years ago. Jake glanced at his new pair of orange and blue shoes that were now an indistinguishable shade of brown, although the color wasn't on his mind at the moment; rather it was on the weight of the shoes with a layer of mud now caked around them.

After a few deep breaths Jake took a spot where the white chalk line had been before the rains came. The two oak trees—not the official starting line by any means--would have to be the symbolic starting line on a day some would describe as 'not fit for man nor beast.' The rain seemed to gain momentum as the starter gave the commands to start the race.

'On your marks...GO!' And just like that, the runners were off, virtually impossible for spectators to see a mere 100 yards into the race due to the blanket of rain that continued to fall from the sky.

Jake ran comfortably for the first lap, remembering the words of Terry Bowers about the course being tricky. With the rain continuing to fall, visibility was difficult. Fortunately Jake was able to see the three or four yards immediately in front of him, allowing him to concentrate on where his next couple of steps would strike the muddy path. One mile into the race two of the runners from Radford were out in front by a couple of seconds; Jake was in a group of five about 20 yards back. Coach Rose caught a glimpse of Jake and the other Blue Harbor runners as they passed through the two oak trees that would now serve as the finish line in two more laps. If it weren't for the bright orange singlets the Herons were wearing there was a very real possibility he wouldn't have noticed them at all. The rain was relentless and visibility was getting worse.

During the second lap Jake made his move. With the same effort he put forth in the first lap he actually lowered his time for the second lap by a couple of seconds, an indication that he was feeling more comfortable with the course after seeing it once. By the time he reached the two oak trees the next time he was leading the race, a couple of strides ahead of Eric Shay and the two runners from Radford.

Jake's confidence was at an all-time high: He was leading the race with one mile left, his friends and family were there to support him (even if he couldn't see them because of the rain) and he could feel JD watching over him and cheering him on. Jake's mind suddenly switched gears. From focusing on what he should be doing at that moment—*'shoulders back, breathe from my stomach, lift my knees, jump over the small puddle two steps from now'*—he began thinking about what might be in store for him down the road. *'Five minutes from now and I'm going to make everyone so proud...'*

Athletes in every sport will tell you theirs is a game of inches and seconds. A game of concentration and focus as well. Runners are no different.

With less than 800 meters—about half a mile remaining in the race Jake was leading his closest competitor by the length of a football field. In fact the runner in second place, Eric Shay could not see Jake as the rain continued to fall.

In fact the rain was now falling so hard Eric Shay wouldn't even notice when he passed Jake Kerslake 400 meters from the finish line.

Neither would all of the other runners in the race as they passed Jake by, one by one.

FORTY-EIGHT – THE TUMBLE

People will tell you when they trip and fall it feels like they're falling in slow motion. In a way it gives the 'life flashing before your eyes' feeling, although not quite as dramatic.

Unless you happen to be Jake Kerslake and you're about a minute from winning the county meet 5-kilometer race and lose your concentration for *just a split-second* and don't notice you're about to step on the side of a mud puddle with your still fragile ankle and your foot buckles and you take a nose dive into the deep grass on the side of the path in the middle of one of the worst rain storms in the history of Blue Harbor. Because then it most certainly IS a life-flashing-before-your-eyes moment.

Jake knew better. It had been taught, no *preached* to him all season long. *'Run with your head.'* The words reverberated inside his head as he floated—at least it felt that way to him—in slow motion to the ground. Mental images of rescuing Maui the cat from a tree on the lawn of the house next door, Tim Pittsinger and the Brat Pack chasing after him, running down a purse snatcher on Founder's Way, Coach Rose giving him two cross-country uniforms, kissing Jessica on the front porch, playing with the kids at Best Foot Forward and accompanying JD for his first run in 50 years flickered through his mind in the second-and-a-half it took from tripping to ending up face down in the grass.

It wasn't only Eric Shay who didn't notice Jake lying in the grass while running by. None of the other four dozen runners saw him either. Coach Rose, standing by one of the oak trees wasn't surprised to see a runner in an orange uniform cross the finish line first. He was surprised however that it was Eric Shay and not Jake Kerslake. He was even more surprised that none of the next four Blue Harbor Herons to cross the finish line were either.

One can only imagine what went through Coach Rose's mind when the last runner crossed the finish line and Jake Kerslake was still nowhere in sight.

FORTY-NINE — GRAND FINALE

I t was the first time all morning that Jake noticed how cold the raindrops were as they pelted his prone body on the wet grass. Angry at first for falling in the most important race of the year, the anger quickly transitioned to disappointment before finally turning into complete resignation. There was no need for Jake to finish; winning the county five-kilometer championship was no longer a possibility.

That thought was short-lived, however when Jake remembered JD's note: *Most of all remember to always put your best foot forward in everything you do.* The words were vivid…clear…almost *haunting.* Then Jake thought about the hardships and obstacles his friends at Best Foot Forward faced every single day of their lives. *'Who am I to give up just because of a silly little fall? Lying on my back and feeling sorry for myself is not putting my best foot forward. What would Mikey think? Or Dylan? Melissa? Miss B? Jessica? Tim? Coach Rose? My teammates?* **JD?** *Good lord:* **What would JD think?** *I have to get up and finish this race. I have GOT to give it my best, even if it means finishing last.' Jake couldn't get the thought of his run with JD last week out of his mind— in rain just as ferocious as todays— and how JD wanted to finish the run simply because it wasn't his nature to quit.*

Jake had to use both arms to get to his feet, so it's understandable why he failed to notice how badly he had reinjured his ankle…or that his left arm was covered in blood, a result of his left shoulder striking a rather large rock when he hit the ground. Rather, his thoughts were focused on how comforting it was to have the support of so many people…so many *good* people who were now in his life. People that prior to three months ago he didn't even know existed. Yet today they were an integral part of each and every day. They were his friends; better yet, friends who truly cared about him.

Those thoughts comforted Jake; then suddenly instinct took over and he struggled to get to his feet. No matter what, he decided, he was going to cross that finish line. Despite his cold, aching body and every other runner having already finished the race, Jake ran those final 400 meters with the determination and effort of a young man you would expect to see out in front of all the other runners…not more than 10 minutes behind the last runner to finish.

Jake was met with a thunderous ovation worthy of the winner of the Olympic Marathon—something he would one day realize first hand--from those who stuck around in the pouring rain to watch all the runners finish. They were glad they did, because had they left they'd have missed out on the opportunity to see Jake Kerslake cross the finish line with a smile on his face as wide as the Mississippi River. It was a smile of satisfaction; satisfaction in knowing that, on this particular day under the most difficult circumstances Jake had covered the path in front of him to the best of his ability.

Those who didn't stick around missed something else as well: A rainbow once the rain finally came to a halt.

As Jake glanced at the magnificent spectrum of colors in the sky he couldn't help but take it as a sign from above that he accomplished what he set out to do.

There was no doubt in Jake's mind. The rainbow was a sign from JD telling him that he was very, very proud of him because on this difficult, trying day Jake Kerslake had found a way to put his best foot forward.

FIFTY – FADE TO WHITE

L ater that same day Blue Harbor experienced the latest spring snowfall in its history. Several inches of pure white powder blanketed the ground, providing the perfect complement to the gray and cloudy skies overhead. Virtually everything in Blue Harbor was covered in snow, creating a beautiful backdrop for next year's Christmas cards.

The city was literally covered in a blanket of white, except for a certain bench in the middle of Central Park with a pair of orange and blue orange shoes draped over one end.

The bench, of course was the former residence of one Jefferson Saine Douglas.

Or JD, as he was known by all of his friends.

EPILOGUE

.... ──────────────────────────────

S andy Bowers realized one of her dreams when an additional wing was added to Best Foot Forward. In it were six additional activity rooms, two complete bathrooms, a small library (with four computers!) and an exercise room. More importantly a lot of deserving lives were positively impacted, thanks to one last generous donation to BFF left in the will of Jefferson Saine.

Blue Harbor Senior High went on to win the county meets for the next three years. Eric Shay repeated as the five-kilometer champion the year after winning it as a freshman and Jake Kerslake would win it the two years after that.

Coach Bill Rose remained at Blue Harbor Junior High another three years as head coach of the cross-country team. He stood behind Jake Kerslake and Eric Shay as they both signed full athletic scholarships at the nearby state university. After retirement Bill Rose traveled to as many of Jake and Eric's collegiate meets as his schedule allowed, squeezing it between all of the things he 'always wanted to do,' although everyone knew that what he really wanted to do was coach running.

Tim Pittsinger, after repeating ninth grade would graduate and sign an athletic scholarship to throw the shot put. Many thought he had the potential to compete in the Olympics someday. When Tim graduated from high school his sister Tina was in the front row of the gymnasium, a seat she chose intentionally so that people sitting behind her wouldn't see her crying. It didn't matter to her if Tim saw her crying; after all she wanted him to know how proud she was of him. He was becoming the person she always knew he was capable of being.

Mikey and Dylan, just as Melissa had before them went on to be contributing members of society. Mikey bagged groceries three days a week at the largest grocery store in town and on weekends worked on various landscaping projects for the good people of Blue Harbor, the latter fueled by his reputation as having the greenest thumb in town. Dylan wrote two columns a week for the local newspaper, mostly human interest stories consisting of some of the most inspiring words one could ever hope to run across. Dylan also helped Melissa plan activities for the children at Best Foot Forward a couple of nights a week at the request of Miss B.

Jake would eventually marry his childhood sweetheart. No one was surprised by Jake's selection of Tim Pittsinger as his best man. Melissa was in the wedding party; so were Mikey and Dylan. The wedding was one the people of Blue Harbor would talk about for years to come. Sandy Bowers sang; those in attendance said she sang with the voice of an angel. The wedding took place on a crisp, cool fall afternoon in Central Park. The ceremony was performed on a small platform constructed specifically for the occasion, positioned next to a certain red bench where the squirrels were once fed on a regular basis. The entire wedding party wore matching orange and blue tennis shoes…just like the ones still hanging on one end of the park bench.

ABOUT THE AUTHOR

Scott Ludwig was born in Norfolk, Virginia. As a child his family was asked to relocate every three years by his father's employer, the United States Navy.

Scott has written 11 books, all nonfiction. This, his 12th book is his first attempt at fiction. It is also his first try at writing for a younger audience. Since he was young at one time, he considers himself an expert on the subject. Feel free to judge for yourself.

Scott and his wife Cindy live in Senoia, Georgia. They have two sons, one grandson, three cats and a six-foot alligator that stands guard over their 1.8-acre property they call 'the Swamp.'

If you ever cross paths with Scott he'll be glad to connect the dots between the people, places and things in this book and the people, places and things in his life. Just allow yourself a couple of hours to get through all of them.

And if you happen to bring your copy of this book with you, there's a pretty good chance he'll sign it for you.

If you want him to, of course.

ABOUT THE COVER ARTIST

Marjorie Bowers is a resident of Lilburn, Georgia but as an avid RVer, she and her husband Carl spend a considerable amount of time traveling all over the United States seeking out unique subject matter to photograph for later use in her drawings. She spends a considerable amount of time getting the photo 'just right,' sometimes photographing at different times of the day to get the best shadows and light.

While pen and inks create the exquisite details, Marjorie also incorporates pencil when the subject matter calls for a more relaxed feel or some extra depth. Quite often she will choose an area to treat with 'isolated color,' highlighting an area with a dramatic flair.

Marjorie has no formal background in arts and works on instinct. Though she had finished a few drawings along the way, her true love affair with the pen was ignited following the tragic loss of her youngest child in 2005. Using art as therapy, by 2011 she had enough work to take the leap of faith and became a full time artist. Her drawings have won national awards and are featured in numerous art galleries.

Marjorie incorporated a letter 'K' with a shamrock hidden in all of her drawings from 2005 through 2014 in honor of her daughter Kelly when tragedy struck again and she lost her beautiful stepdaughter, Sandy. Now she also includes a heart broken with the letter 'S' as her heart was truly broken when Sandy left her much too soon.

Sandy lit a torch in the Bowers family with her ever-present smile and gregarious laugh. A single mother, Sandy raised a daughter Allison who keeps that torch lit and has become quite the inspirational woman herself.

ABOUT THE ILLUSTRATOR

JaRodney Anderson was born in Macon, Georgia and raised in Jeffersonville, a small rural town of less than 2,000 and only one traffic light. He currently lives in Palmetto, Georgia and is the proud father of three beautiful children, daughters Aaliyah and Jordan and son Jaylen.

During his Junior High School years JaRodney played football as a wide receiver. He discovered his talent for drawing much earlier: At the age of six.

JaRodney never expressed a desire in learning to draw; rather, it *just happened...like magic.'* It's something he enjoys doing and claims it *feels right'* when he does. His talent was recognized by the faculty and students of his school system and today he has thousands of people following his artistic creations on social media.

> *'With my artwork, I hope to allow people to escape reality and look through the eyes of others in so many different ways.'*

It is the author's hope and intent that this book will do just that.

> *To see more of JaRodney's art, you can find him on Instagram at:*
> art_work_in_the_basement

The character in this book named Sandy Bowers was inspired by the real Sandy Bowers, the late daughter of the woman responsible for the wonderful artwork on the front cover.

The Sandy Bowers Memorial Scholarship Foundation

Sandy Bowers was a beautiful and bright woman with child-like energy, a generous heart and an empathetic ear. Sandy wanted sobriety and all the unconditional gifts that came along with it, perhaps more than anyone else. Nonetheless, Sandy lost her long battle with addiction in March of 2014.

This Memorial Scholarship Fund was established by Sandy's family to allow women who greatly want the gift of sobriety the opportunity for long-term treatment at Lee Street Recover (www.leestreetrecovery.com) in Statesboro, Georgia. Lee Street is where Sandy found sobriety in 2010 and according to her family was amongst the happiest years of her life.

Our hope is you find it in your heart to make a donation to this wonderful charity.

The Sandy Bowers Memorial Scholarship Fund
P.O. Box 1011
Statesboro, Georgia 30459

ACKNOWLEDGEMENTS

I would like to personally thank **Marjorie Bowers** and **JaRodney Anderson** for their help 'bringing this book to life' through their amazing pencil drawings.

Marjorie, I appreciate the addition of the pair of shoes to one of your original drawings for the sake of this book cover. I wish you continued success with your art in the future. May more and more people have the opportunity to see your work in person so they can be as mesmerized by it as I have been since the day I first saw it at an art festival in Atlanta, Georgia several years ago. My wife and I are proud to have several of your works in various places throughout our home, and hope to add more in the years ahead.

JaRodney, I hope your work in this book will serve as a stepping stone for you in promoting and developing your talent as an artist. I am proud to feature your art in the pages of this book so others will have the chance to 'escape reality and see the world through the eyes of others,' as you so aptly put it.

I would also like to thank **Susanne Thurman** for lending her support in the finer points of formatting the manuscript, converting the works of Ms. Bowers and Mr. Anderson into printable material and handling all of the other technical aspects that were above my pay grade.

This book wouldn't be possible without the three of you.

Scott Ludwig
Senoia, Georgia
August 2016

Printed in the United States
By Bookmasters